AN EVIL WAS BORN

I0599084

MIRIKA MAYO CORNELIUS

author of best-selling novels Curse the Cotton and The
Secret Novel Collection

AN EVIL WAS BORN

Copyright © Mirika Mayo Cornelius, October 2018
ISBN: 978-1-946870-07-0

An Akirim Press Publishing
Book Cover by Akirim Press/Mirika Mayo Cornelius
www.akirimpress.com

<u>Acknowledgements</u>

I first and always thank God for the giving of his Son, Jesus, to save me, and I acknowledge and confess that without Him, I have and am nothing.

I love you, son. Forever.

mirikacornelius.com

AN EVIL WAS BORN

After a tragic loss, a young couple discovers something sinister that has entered their home, and it's toying with their daughter. Will they be able to hold on to their faith and save their family, or will fear take such a solid grip on their lives that the silent intruder becomes unstoppable?

TABLE OF CONTENTS

AN EVIL WAS BORN

PROLOGUE

"What's wrong, baby? Stop screaming now and tell me what's wrong! Open the door, Macon!" He shoved desperately against the bathroom door of her father's home. "Macon!" he shouted, unable to get the door open as the screams continued to penetrate beyond the solid, brown door into the hallway. He'd heard her screaming from outside and rushed inside, away from the small cookout that was going on out back. Many outside watched as he burst into the home, but they didn't know why as they were dancing and having such a good time before his eruption. He was the only one close enough to the house at the time to hear her screams over the music.

"What's happening?" she wailed in a tone terrified enough to wake the sleeping from their graves. "Jesus, please!"

"Macon!" Finally, he hit the door so hard that it flew open, and he stumbled through, distraught at what he saw once inside the small space. His wife was crouched against the sink, beholding something that looked human but smaller than what would be a normal size. At the sight, he fell to his knees, and without hesitation, wrapped his hand around the life that had fallen beneath his distraught wife. "Somebody help us! Help us, please!" he called, straining with every bit of his strength that was coiled up in his veins.

His wife quickly lost all of her strength, passing out directly over him, as he held on to the only life they had ever made together. With his other arm, he caught her mid-fall, and there he remained with his young wife in one arm and his newborn baby in the palm of his hand as the blood circled his legs and feet. Of the three, only two survived.

SUNNI'S BIRTH

"Look, look, Macon!" he shouted as the child began to come from his wife's womb.

"I can't look. I'm pushing, so leave me alone. Just leave me be. Can you put him out of here? Please," she begged as tears rolled down her high cheekbones and her fists clenched the legs of the bed while her father's neighbor nervously shrugged her shoulders and asked if he could leave out.

"She's right. Just go wait out on the porch for the midwife. Make sure she gets the right house. My house is open," she suggested, hoping he would go sit there and wait instead of parading around his laboring wife creating more of a panic. "Call my husband again, Greg, at his job. The number is on the phone in the kitchen. You can't miss it." She wiped her forehead as she slid on the thick, yellow gloves that she got from underneath the kitchen sink. "Are you sure these are clean enough?" she asked the straining woman while she adjusted the phone on her ear the best way she could as the phone's cord continued to wrap her in a bind.

"I don't care, Ms. Margaret. I just don't. They're the gloves my dad keeps there. Please," she cried, "This baby is killing me."

"Go call *your* husband and wait on a midwife?" Greg interjected. "And what do I need your husband for? This is *my* baby, not your husband's!" Greg retorted. "She said she's about to die. Didn't you hear her? Look…give me the gloves and the phone and you go out and look for your own husband and direct the midwife wherever she is." He reached over and snatched the phone while she looked on in horror with her hands in the air. "I'll take those, too," he exclaimed, snatching the gloves from off her hands. "This is *my* baby," he explained with a great, big grin. "Come on out to daddy, baby. I gotcha."

"Macon, he's taking over." She ran out with tears in her eyes, completely exhausted and frustrated by the last thirty minutes of her life but trying not to complain because the woman with the expanded vaginal hole and a head pushing through it seemed far more in need of relief than her. "I can't take this anymore. This shouldn't be happening…"

"Give her back the gloves!" the laboring woman yelled.

"No! Now you sit back and push when you feel a contraction. I've been asking around about this day, and I know one thing, you push at the contraction. You got to push him out, Macon," he stated, assuming his child was going to be a boy, "because I'm not pulling. I might hurt something."

"I'm pushing! Is *she* not moving? Her head should be out by now. Something's wrong. Put your hand in there to make sure the cord isn't around her neck," she ordered as he sat there gawking like a stunned child at the request. "Do it!"

"Just stick my hand in there?" he yelled frantically.

"You stick everything else in there, so why not?" she exaggerated in frustration and agony. "Just get my baby!"

"Hello. Hello! I'm here." A tall, stocky woman entered the home, pouring sweat while dropping to her knees directly beside Greg.

"I have to stick my hand in my wife's vagina because she said she's pushing, but the baby isn't coming out. Some talk about the cord on the baby's neck."

"If you need to check the cord, we need to put our hands into the vagina and you will feel it," she responded, grabbing Greg's hand and removing the glove so that she can take over. "The distress more than likely isn't coming from the cord, sir, if she is feeling any. If in fact the cord is around the neck of the child, we'll simply remove it from the neck, if we can."

"I can get some scissors…"

"No you don't. Cut the cord after the baby is out. Not like this. We gonna get it out. Not to worry. I been doing this a long time."

"Easy for you to say. Hold still, Macon. Just hold still. Breathe. You certain you can't get up from here?" the older woman asked, looking around in the room as if something was the matter.

"What's wrong with the baby? What's wrong? It shouldn't be this hard, Greg, and no! Does it look like I can move right now?" she panted in extreme anguish.

"I don't think her hands are gonna fit in there," he continued fearfully frustrated but focused, believing that the midwife may hurt the infant as it exited her old home into a new way of living. "Her hands are too big, Macon. Her hands are way too big. This woman is bigger than me, so I don't see how…"

"What? That makes no sense! Oh God, here comes another one," she groaned while pushing her hardest until the baby's head was completely hanging out and propped up by the midwife.

"Oh, Jesus. Oh dear, Lord God, forgive me for my sins. Macon, I'm not gonna make it. I'm not gonna make it," he whined, the sweat pouring from his face, neck and arms like he was squirted with a water hose.

"Greg, please!" she screamed as he stood there gawking at the woman with his child's head in his hands, believing with all his heart that the baby was choking to death on Macon's vaginal wall.

"You got to open up some more. Her head is hanging out, Macon. Open up!" he shouted, already at his wit's end with seeing his baby squished in what looked like an undersized gap.

"I got no control over this and how wide it gets! Is that what you think? Oh, Greg, please leave!"

"Macon, I don't know what to think! All I know is that the neck is in your vagina, and the baby ain't coming out! Now push," he exclaimed as soon as doors slam outside of his window. He looked up to see relief as the small ambulance showed up finally to help deliver his newborn.

"While you were doing all that hollering," stated the calm midwife, wiping out the infant's mouth, "You missed this last part here. Congratulations. Here *she* is. Now go get those scissors…and hurry up. We got to get her out of here," she uttered fearfully as she covered the bloody newborn underneath her clothing like it was her own child. Then, she stared at Macon sorrowfully. "We got to get her from this side quickly."

‖

"Look at her, Greg. Just look at her. See what I did," she laughed in immutable joy as he stared on while his newborn baby girl nursed on her mother's nipple.

"I see what *we* did," he stressed with a grin so wide and strong, proud of his child. "And

15

she's alive," he whispered to himself, not realizing that she heard him, reminding Macon of their past loss, a loss he had yet to fully recover from. "How does she know how to do that? You didn't even teach her yet?"

"It's God given instinct, Greg," she responded, thankful that he didn't linger on their past loss too long so that they could both enjoy their new blessing...their brand new start. It was hard enough for her to move forward after the loss, but she forced herself to do so. If she didn't, everything would have fallen apart. She had to be the glue. "She knows where to get everything she needs right now. She knows our voices and our scents, mine better than yours right now, but you wait until you start holding her a bit. She knows. She knows."

Macon's curly, dark brown hair was pulled up in a pony tail as she smiled and leaned down slightly to place a forehead kiss on her soft and precious newborn. As she closed her eyes and smelled the nice, new scent of her child, the hospital room door opened and a husky, familiar voice called.

"Where's that grandchild of mine? I missed the whole thing, but I got here as soon as I could."

"Daddy?" Macon called surprised as she sat up straighter in the bed. She was shocked to see him make it to the hospital so soon.

"Pops Macon, come on in here…and she's a beauty, too," Greg responded, pushing his chest out like he was the one who carried her for the whole nine months.

"Well, you know what they say." He walked inside, leaning back like a boxer with both his fists in front of his face before playfully punching his son-n-law in the shoulder.

"No fruit talking, daddy. I must admit though, the apple doesn't fall far from the tree. We do have good genes."

"Sure do, and that ain't gonna change. Smart as whips, good looking, and sure about ourselves in every way. Your mama side is good looking, too. Can't say much else."

"Daddy! Come on now. If Ma was living still, she would have popped you in the mouth," she grinned.

"Yeah, but I sure hate she missed this."

"She's not missing it, daddy. She has a really good view from up there. Better than all of us."

"What's her name? And give me that baby when she's done on you."

"Her name is Sunni, with the letter I instead of Y. Sorry for the mess, but she was born right there in your house. I couldn't make it out," she smiled. "Some visit, huh?"

"In the house, Macon?" he stumbled, feeling a bit uneasy, before clearing his throat. "I didn't know," he stuttered again, shaken by what she said but quickly letting it all leave his mind. "I got the call from a friend of mine and came on up here. Nobody told me where they got you from. I hadn't even been back home yet," he stated before digressing back to his new grandbaby. "But that's right fine of you, naming her after your mother. She looks just like the both of you," he continued, moving the chair right beside his thirty-two year old daughter. "I'm glad you chose to honor your mother. She was a fine lady. I sure miss her."

"Here you go, daddy. She's done now. Hold your Sunni again, but this time, she's your sweet granddaughter."

As he took her into his arms, he held her closely, being reminded of the gift of life, and then, just as fast as the beautiful day came in, the sun began to set. The night came in, and it became one of the darkest nights on record.

CHAPTER 2

"It's never the right time, Greg," she complained. "We still need another car. We have enough money saved, and I'm tired of being scared to believe in something more, especially now, and not moving toward the mark. We can't always prepare for rainy days to come. We have to prepare and make way for more good times, too."

"Listen, Macon. We just saved up that money, and I don't want to blow it on more motorized wheels when we can walk or ride by foot on a bicycle. Sunni is our second chance here, remember? The first time, we didn't have anything. No house, no car no nothing to put her in. I want to do right with this second chance. I want to save every dime I can, even if it means my own self being without for the rest of my life." He put on his shoes and began fixing his work clothes before Macon interjected what she knew was going to be a long, drawn out speech that she couldn't care less to hear.

"We have lots of life left, baby. Sunni is only five, and by the time we pay for another car, there will be plenty more where that came from. I'm thirty-seven, and there is no chance we can have more children anyway according to the doctor, so everything will be there for Sunni anyway so…"

"No!" he shouted, but regretted yelling immediately afterward after watching his wife jump in fear because he rarely, if ever, raised his voice at her. He apologetically reached to touch her waist, and she allowed him to do so, realizing that he was sorry about his tone. She already knew it was tough to get him out of the mindset of loss and losing since the death of their first born. "Listen, Macon. This is my only daughter, your only daughter. We lost the first one, and it took years for us to get another baby, another blessing. She's growing good, and I guess I'm just scared because…"

"Something could go wrong."

He let her go and moved away while wiping the back of his neck, his muscles protruding through his shirt due to the overwhelming amount of stress he'd put himself under, constantly concerning himself with having a backup plan and backup money. It was a looming cloud over their heads for a long while. Perfection in life never lasted long it seemed, but they were always able to overcome the challenges that may have strangled them to death. The worst of it came in the 1955 when they thought they would have their first child, but then came her death. He wasn't the same man she'd met and fallen in love with, and his severely distressed spirit lasted for one whole year. His moods would swing out of control, and he hated everything he saw, especially himself, blaming himself that he couldn't save his own child. That was when good became bad all at once. Nothing was guaranteed, and they began to feel that they even caused bad to come from having good expectations. From there, everything they did was in preparation for something horrible to happen instead of simply living life until something bad actually did happened. They'd started to search for the bad, even in the good.

"Yeah. Doesn't it always go wrong? I mean, you've been right here with me. We've been together. No matter how hard we both try, we get set back. Even when the worst day of my life…" he trembled, but she stopped his train of thought before he went back there to get captured in it once again.

"But this time we aren't set back. Here we are, twelve years later since we lost our first child, and we have a five year old, beautiful baby girl. I think it's time, Greg, to start believing things are on the up and up from now on. We need a car. I need to get around while you're a work, too. Sunni is about to start school, and I need to get back to work during the day." She approached him as he leaned against the old, oak dresser that sat there doing its job, even with two cracked drawers and an uneven floor to hold it up. "Thank you for everything. You're doing a great job, but I can help financially now. I can...if only for six months to a year."

"Who's gonna watch Sunni after school?" he asked, concerned about his daughter's well-being.

"Me. Me, baby. Me, okay? I will be here. I won't take a job unless I can be home with her. Now, I really would like for you to see things my way, but even if you don't," she paused, standing as firm as she could on her desires, "I'm going to work. I need a car," she stressed, her eyes pleading with him for understanding. "Get us one."

After a brief silence and hearing her case for many times over, he finally gave in to her demands. "I hear you. I'll...I guess I'll stop by the lot, and see if that old man has a car, a small, inexpensive one, that we can get with the money that I've saved up."

Her eyes lit up. "Thank you! You'll find it. It doesn't have to be expensive, as long as it has four wheels on it and some doors and lights and operates, it'll be good. And don't worry. I already spoke to a few people about a job, and I'm expecting a call back anytime."

"That's why you've been off the phone, I see."

"Yes." She clapped her hands together and then gave him a huge kiss on his lips. "The only conversation I want to have on that phone is one with an employer who wants to hire me."

"I hear you. Well, good luck. I'm off to work."

"No luck. Prayers. We live off of faith in this house. No more bad times."

"Yeah...I hear you," he hesitated, realizing that he was just upbeat to keep a smile on her face. He still had that same nagging sensation that the devil had more tricks hidden and ready to use as a wrench in their future, therefore, he couldn't let loose of all his paranoia, not wanting to be on the losing end again.

"You'll see," she called behind him as he exited the bedroom, shaking his head like he didn't know what he was getting himself into. When she heard the front door slam shut, she leaned out the bedroom window. "Watch, Greg. Just watch."

"I am watching," he laughed. "My eyes are wide open and staring right into my wallet. But hey, you might just be right this time."

"I am, baby. I am. I can feel it." The phone started to ring. "There's the phone! Bye!" She didn't wait to watch him drive off before she was already running into the kitchen to answer it. "Hello?" When she didn't get an answer, she anxiously continued speaking in a professional tone believing that it was a potential job offer, forgetting that it was too early in the morning for an employer's call. "This is Mrs. McKinsey."

"I know who this is. How you been?"

"Who is this?"

"This is your cousin, Braille. You don't recognize my voice anymore? It's been that long?"

"Braille? Is this really you?" she asked in shock. "I thought you were still in the hospital. Are you out? I was gonna catch the bus to come see you up there today."

"I got out last night, and when I got home, I went straight to bed."

"And how are you feeling?"

"I'm good enough to be out of the hospital. I'll be back to work soon, but I need to ask you a favor until then because they told me to rest on doctor's orders."

"Go ahead," Macon responded as she waved her freshly waking daughter to her side. The child stumbled over to her and cradled it like it was a pillow while nodding back off to sleep standing up.

"I need only a couple of dollars to get by on food since I won't be able to work, and I don't have anything saved up and with the bill from the hospital, I'm all out of money just that fast. Can you help me with that? I'm getting other help, but I don't feel right asking one person for a large lump sum of money. I prefer to get a couple of dollars from everyone until I can function and get another check from the job."

"Say no more. I have some money saved. I can spare a few dollars, and you don't have to pay me back. How's that? Plus, I can always bring you a plate after I cook here at the house," she insisted.

Macon and her first cousin had been through much together as children. As a matter of fact, it was because of Braille that Macon rarely had to stand up for herself in the first place. Although they didn't grow up in the same town after she left with her parents as a little girl, she would visit all the time. Any enemy of Macon's was an enemy of hers.

Braille was a stocky, young girl, bigger than some boys, and the last person anyone wanted to mess with was her. She was afraid of no one except her own father, but when both her parents passed away when she was just a teen, she took on the work of a man to support herself. It was because of this, that some men didn't like her much. Even though she was rough around the edges and liable to get confused in her head over simple things at times, she missed the one thing she wanted most of all - to fall in love with a good man. They would always overlook her though, believing that she was too strong, intimidating, and even a bit odd, but in reality, she was the most weak at heart when it came down to her fantasies about marrying the man of her dreams.

There was a time when she got all dolled up with Macon when they were both twenty-four years old and went out to a small club on the other side of town just to have fun. Of course, Macon was engaged at the time, so she wasn't looking for herself, however, Braille was determined to attract the attention of a handsome man.

||

"Now, Braille, you have to calm down."

"I am calm."

"No, I mean, just calm down. Let the man be the man, okay? They like to actually be the man in the relationship, you know," she joked.

"Oh I know. I'm just so used to doing everything on my own so much that I just don't know how to relax. It's automatic."

"Your guard is up. Let me handle that. I have a man, so I can be your guard this time."

Braille eyeballed her scrawny cousin, and then laughed, "No, you definitely can't defend me from a gnat, much less a crazy, bull-headed man."

"Well, I'll try. Listen though. Greg took me to this place a couple of times before when I was nineteen, so we go in, sit and wait. You look nice. You'll see. Don't look for them either. Let them do the looking."

That was the most hopeful conversation they had because as soon as they got inside, a man reached to touch Braille on her backside and the next thing that happened was a full fist across the perpetrator's mouth. Needless to say, they left, holding their stomachs and laughing back to the car that hadn't even started getting cold in the parking lot. They both agreed – he deserved it.

||

"I knew I could count on you. Even though you claim I don't have to pay you back, I will. Trust me, Macon, I will."

"As much as you've done for me? No you don't."

"I sure will. Thanks, Macon. I love you so much. If I didn't have you, I'd have no one. How's Sunni?"

"She's good. Just woke up and going right back to sleep on my leg. Listen, I'm waiting on an important phone call, so whenever Greg gets back home, I will bring you the money. Just don't tell Greg. Money is going to be tight until I get a job," she stated, failing to reveal her push to get a new vehicle.

"I won't," she laughed. "Thank you."

"Bye." She hung up the telephone and then leaned over to kiss the top of her child's head. "Good morning, beautiful. Come on. Wake up. Mama's thigh isn't your pillow anymore. You're too big."

"I want something to eat," the little girl whined as she woke up just enough to hold her mother's hand and walk to the kitchen where she took a seat at the kitchen table. "Where's my food?"

"Sunni, now. Don't start this morning. We have gone over this many times, just about every single morning. I'm not cooking food to just have it sit on the stove until you decide to wake up. You know how you are, only hungry when you don't see the food. When you do see it, you're not hungry," she stated as she put on her apron. "You have to get out of that, too, you know, because you'll be starting school, and I'm going back to work. Now sit," she commanded, pointing to the kitchen table. "It won't take but two minutes to get this done."

The child placed her head on the table and shut her eyes as her mother cracked the eggs to put them in the frying pan. As soon as the eggs hit the pan, the sizzle sound made its unique buzz all around the kitchen. Usually when Macon made eggs, she fried bologna with it. Then, she would lightly toast some bread, and when everything was finished cooking, she would sandwich everything inside. This was what she did this particular morning.

The meal didn't take long at all to cook, and once she was finished, she went to place the food onto Sunni's plate. However, when she turned around, Sunni was missing from the table. Confused but not upset, she called for her but got no answer. After calling a couple times to only get no response, she removed her apron, set the food onto the table, sighed and headed down the hallway.

"She must be in the bathroom. Sunni, you need some help in there, sweetheart? Don't put the toothpaste all over the counter, alright?" When she turned the knob on the bathroom door, the door swung open, but there was no Sunni. "Sunni? That girl went back to sleep, just like I thought she would," she smiled, before she heard knocking. "Sunni?"

The knocking was coming from the master bedroom, so that was where she headed. Peeping in, she saw nothing, however, she still heard the noise. "Sunni, is that you?" She moved toward the other side of her bed where she found Sunni destroying the wall that her dad had already patched up just two days ago. "Sunni!"

"I want some food!" the child screamed. "I told you I want some food! Give it to me."

"Sunni, stop it! What has gotten into you? Have you lost your mind, huh?" she asked, awaiting a reply from her daughter. She snatched Sunni up from the floor while gawking in disbelief at the new hole Sunni kicked back into the wall. "What would make you do something like that? You know your father just fixed this wall! Go to your room now!" Macon dropped to the floor to try and pack the wall back together, but as she wiped up the shattered fragments, she noticed Sunni standing over her glaring, fists clenched and breathing like a child about to have a temper tantrum. "Didn't I tell you to go to your room, Sunni? Do it now!" she shouted only to be answered with an unexpected kick to the stomach.

A horror-struck Macon clenched her stomach and drew back in disbelief at what Sunni did. It was then that Sunni ran off into her room and slammed the door, leaving her mother squeezing at the sheets of the bed in pain. It took Macon a minute to rise from the floor. The kick was directly in the spot where she'd had surgery only one year ago, and she felt the jolt of pain right at her kidney. Shaken by the events that just occurred, she stood as quickly as she could and located a belt before stomping down the hall and to Sunni's room. "This ain't nothing that a spanking can't handle," she stressed, holding back tears but ready to handle things the way they'd always been handled in her family. Sunni never had a spanking before, not one day in her life.

"Sunni! Take your clothes off now and let me see your naked behind. Lean over on that bed, child, right now!" She burst through the door imagining she would see Sunni hiding at the thought of being punished, but instead, she saw her under the covers and back to sleep. Momentarily, she stopped, confused at the sight, but then she marched to the bed, threw back the cover and shook the sleeping child awake. "Get up. You're not asleep! Wake up, Sunni. You don't ever hit nor kick me…ever!"

Just then, as if she'd never been awake, Sunni woke up to her mom shouting over her body, causing her to scurry to the other side of the bed in pure fear. "Mama! Stop it! You scaring me."

Macon, although she had the belt ready, holding it high in the air, quickly put it behind her back. Something was wrong, and she knew it. Terror blinded her child's young eyes, and the sweet child that had never known fear a day in her life became held in its clutches as her body begged the wall behind her for protection.

"No, no, baby," Macon called as the belt dropped from her hand and onto the floor. The sound of the buckle hitting the floor caused another panic in Sunni that made her jump into a frenzied scream once again. "Nothing's wrong, baby. Come here, now, come on. I thought something happened. I didn't even know it was you in the bed. I thought...I thought it was somebody else," she lied. "Come here."

"It's me, Mama. It's me," she cried, holding out her arms, flipping them over in order to prove it was her.

Macon crawled onto the bed, and Sunni finally moved toward her as well. When they connected, it was as if they hadn't seen each other in years. Macon squeezed her tightly, forgetting all about the kick she and the crumbled wall endured. Her only concern was why Sunni couldn't remember a thing about what she'd done just minutes ago.

"Hey," Macon began as she lifted Sunni from the bed with a huge smile on her face, desiring to get back to a happy morning. "Let's go eat breakfast."

"You cooked already?"

The question tore through Macon's heart, but she remained calm while Sunni stared back at her waiting for an answer while wiping the tears from her baby eyes.

"Yeah," Macon whispered, quickly smiling even wider to mask her dismay. "Yeah, sure did. I made some eggs and fried bologna.

Don't you like that?" she asked, placing Sunni on the floor and reaching for her daughter's hand as they walked from the bedroom.

"Yep. But I have to brush my teeth first. I'll be back."

Macon felt Sunni's hand slip away from hers, and she watched as she ran down the short hallway into the bathroom. Suddenly afraid for her to be alone, she waited impatiently for the sound of running water. When she heard it, tears flowed from her eyes, and she held her heart before asking, "What just happened to my baby?"

With every sound coming from the bathroom, she traced Sunni's movements to make certain they were in order. She even strained to hear her breathing, spitting and even washing her face. Although everything sounded like the normal, everyday routine of things, she knew something was off schedule. There was something else inside the house that changed when the sun rose that morning that wasn't there before. It terrified her, and she wanted it to leave instantly. It reminded her of all the bad that tended to fog their lives every time things were going well, but she'd already decided to not give, what she considered the devil, a stronghold. She was going to fight.

"Lord, send it away," she prayed as she stood there in the hallway staring at the bathroom door. Her hands trembled, and her throat could barely get the words out, but she continued to repeat the short, yet direct, prayer to her Only Help. "Lord, please, I don't know what's wrong, but I don't want to know. I need you to know and fix it right now before it takes hold. Amen." She'd never been taught to believe in old time superstition, but the memories of some of the teachings she was taught to not believe were trying to become real with each second in an attempt to break her faith.

She recalled the old stories she heard when she was little, at her friends' houses, about people who were vexed, and there was one in particular that was about the sleep walker. They would say the devil was walking them around by the head like a puppet, making them go blind, but moving their eyes around like they could had clear vision. Her mother told her those tales weren't true at all, but only passed down as if they were true from the old land. At that moment, Macon had to force that old superstition from her system as she decided to cling to Jesus.

As the bathroom door opened, she turned around quickly and walked toward the kitchen, assuring herself that all was well while hiding her concern from her daughter.

CHAPTER 3

"I smell the food from the front porch. Remember when we nearly burned down Aunt Sunny's house? Hey in there!"

Macon dashed around the corner to come face to face with the person whom she'd been praying for since she was hospitalized. "Braille! Girl, what are you doing over here so early? You should be at home! I just spoke to you. Come on inside. You don't need to stand on the porch, and you know that."

"Well, I wouldn't be standing here if you had the screen door unlocked," she laughed, poking her neck out and frowning her face jokingly.

"Give me a hug!" They embraced, and Macon hollered for her daughter. "Sunni, it's cousin Braille. Come on out here and give her a hug, and don't even remind me of the time we almost burned down my Mama's house. Daddy was about to skin both of us alive."

As Braille stepped inside, Sunni came around the corner with her arms outstretched to hug the cousin she called aunt. "Aunt Braille!" Her arms went around her, but then she backed up puzzled. "You're not big anymore."

"No, I'm not, and hallelujah! The doctor said if that pneumonia didn't kill me then my health was going to do it anyway, so I plan on keeping this weight off me. He said it complicated things, so how do you like me now?" she kidded, twirling around so that they could get a better look. "I figured that I would come by here instead of waiting. A part of resting is getting out and doing what you wanna do, ain't it? It was a short walk."

"Well, I have to tell you, cousin, you look like you never have before. Almost a different lady. Sunni, go back and play a minute, baby."

"Yes ma'am," she responded obediently while her mother and cousin moved into the kitchen.

"Do you want something to eat? Help yourself. You know you're welcome to it."

"Don't mind if I do," she grinned, heading toward the meat. "I still need to keep this weight off. I actually have a waist now, can't you tell?

Macon giggled. "I told you that you've always been a cutie. So, you know I like to play match maker."

"No need. I've had my eyes on one for a long time now, and, Macon, he's so fine. He's a big one, and I know if I stroll in front of him now with my new figure, he won't miss me. Honestly, I think he likes me, too, but I think I have the confidence now."

"You should have had the confidence then," she retorted, disagreeing wholeheartedly with her cousin's normal excuse of her size running men away. "All men don't like the same type of woman just like all women don't like the same type of man. Honestly, if you think he was attracted to you when you were bigger, this may cause him to turn his head to look elsewhere," she laughed.

"Don't say that, Macon," she responded with her eyes bulging from her head. "Come on now. I look better, don't I?" she asked, stretching herself taller, attempting to measure up to Macon's five feet nine inches tall height and slimmer frame.

"Braille." She walked over to touch her cousin on the hand. Braille looked down and placed her other hand atop Macon's. "What have I always told you? Just like my daddy told me. If a man likes you, he likes you. You shouldn't have to change a thing."

"It's just been hard for me, and you know, maybe this new look will help. I want what you and Greg have," she continued, taking a seat with a couple slices of slightly burnt meat, "even a child to call my own."

"Go after him then. Don't have to wait until he sees you. Make him see you, and if he doesn't bite, at least you can allow your heart to move on. Anyway," she continued, peeping down the hallway to make certain Sunni wasn't within sight, "I need to tell you something." She pulled out a chair across from Braille. "Something that happened this morning with Sunni terrified me half to death, so much so that I had to look to the Lord for comfort."

"She looked fine to me. What's so scary about her?"

"It's nothing that you can *see*. She looked fine, but she wasn't fine. It was something different, Braille, and I don't know what to make of it." She paused before beginning again, staring at the dark, wooden table but really listening to be certain that Sunni was still out of sight. "She started destroying the wall where Greg just fixed it the other day. He had a hole there all newly patched up, and she just kicked it all back out! I don't know what I'm gonna tell Greg when he gets home either, but the scariest thing about it is," she continued, leaning forward like she was telling the secret of her life, "she didn't even remember doing it."

Braille stared blankly back at her for about five seconds and then laughed, dismissing everything that she heard. "That child is lying to you. You're falling for those lies already?" Macon wasn't laughing back, and that was when Braille knew there was more to the story.

"She kicked me in my stomach, too. It wasn't a child-being- bad kick, but a real kick. She aimed and fired, right where I'd been injured before, but Braille, she doesn't remember doing that either," she told her cousin, watching her eyes blow up like biscuits in the oven at the words *kicked me in my stomach*. "It's like her soul left, and she became somebody else. You know how we used to talk about how we would get the dead man when we were little?"

"Yeah, how we couldn't move when we'd wake up, and if felt like something was holding us down?" Braille whispered. "It still happens to me sometimes, but it makes me not move."

"Well, the opposite of that. She wasn't sleep walking. I know she wasn't. She answered me and was looking right at me," she whispered, forcefully pointing at herself, "even hugged me on my leg when I was on the phone. She was awake but really wasn't."

"Walking but with the...being led by..."

Not another sound came from Macon's mouth as she shook her head slowly at Braille's words. She knew what Braille was probably thinking, which was the exact same thing that came to her mind, but finally, she spoke up to shut the thought down. "It wasn't what you think. I know what that is. Those old tales are nothing to believe in anyway, right?" When Braille didn't respond, she became more aggressive. "It's not, Braille, I swear, and I'm not lying. I know what they call being led by the devil, but this was different...and I don't believe

in no old tales so don't go putting that on her,"
she rebuked in full denial. "She isn't taken by
any bad spirits."

"Well, let's see. Sunni!" Braille suddenly
hollered angrily, startling Macon, but calling
Sunni in an attempt to put the story to rest.
"Sunni, come here."

"Braille, I'm telling you the truth," she
interrupted, unsure of the tongue lashing she may
give her daughter. "She didn't do it on purpose."

"Kicking you? Kicking you ain't on
purpose? If it ain't a bad spirit, then she is
behaving like a bad girl, and we can figure that
out right now. Sunni, get here right now!" She
stood up from her seat and watched Sunni take
each step toward her while Macon stood back
silently, uncomfortable with it all, but understood
why it may be necessary. It was customary for
family to have the right to discipline family if it
needed to be done. The belief that it took a
village to raise a child was followed as if it came
straight from the Biblical scriptures.

Braille turned to Macon and winked as
Sunni drew closer. That was a relief to Macon as
she knew it meant that it was to scare the truth
out of her more than anything else. "You know

I'm glad to see you, baby cousin, but what did you do to your mama before I got here?" When Sunni glanced away from her without an answer, she shouted, "Answer me!"

Sunni jerked in pure fear and began to cry. The tears broke her mother's heart, and she urged Sunni to tell the truth. Macon, deep down inside, also felt it was necessary to allow a dose of healthy fear to get inside Sunni because she'd been replaying the situation over and over inside her head, but it made no sense. If scaring her into the truth would work, she felt it a good tactic.

"I didn't do nothing to mama. Why you yelling at me? I didn't do nothing," the child cried, finally causing Macon to intervene.

"That's enough, Braille," she said, embracing Sunni to let her know that everything was fine. She then mouthed the words *I told you so* at Braille. Braille nodded in shock, fully aware that most children who lie at that age break under the sound of her loud voice. The revelation also caused her to back away from Sunni slightly before dropping down to apologize.

"Little Sunni, I'm sorry. Cousin made a mistake. I thought you did something to your mom that was really bad," she explained.

"I didn't do anything," Sunni cried.

Braille then asked, "Somebody hurt your mom this morning. You know who did it then?"

Sunni backed away from both of them, and then she looked at her mother sharply at the thought of someone hurting her. "Mama, you should call the police and put them in jail."

At that, Macon and Braille looked at each other and laughed, causing Sunni burst into laughter as well. "Go on back and play, Sunni. Everything is alright."

"Yes ma'am."

As soon as Sunni was down the hallway, Macon's smile disappeared and tears rose up into the lids. "I told you. She doesn't even remember. Now what's that, Braille?"

The smile left Braille's face. She, then, went to wash her hands at the kitchen sink. Macon noticed how Braille had escaped to clean herself off. That was something people did whenever they felt they encountered something evil, even if their hands were clean already, they still re-cleaned them. Macon didn't say a word, although seeing Braille do it broke her heart.

"Are you sure that you didn't lose your own mind? I mean, if she doesn't remember, what if it was you?" Braille asked quietly. "Maybe you're the one being tricked…"

"Me?"

"You. That's what I said." Braille turned to face her, hoping that Macon had imagined it all. "Could it be you?" She pulled the towel from the handle of the oven and began drying her hands so well that by the time she finished they were ashy.

Macon sat down on the chair and rubbed the table lightly with her fingertips. She traced the old, tile flooring with her eyes, going back over every step she took that morning until she looked back up to stare down the hallway. She knew what Braille was doing. She was narrowing it down. The last thing Macon wanted was for anyone to look at Sunni oddly. Therefore, she took the blame.   Even though Braille was family, she knew full well that even family wasn't exempt from harsh feelings about a child that was believed to be vexed. She could tell by the way Braille rushed to wash her hands seconds ago that she would dismiss her faster than a blink if she could convince herself that some foul hex was on her. Nobody wanted to be around that, not even family.

"Maybe. Maybe. What if it was me? I thought about that, too. Whatever. Let's forget about it," she stated as she removed herself from the table and walked Braille to the door after loaning her the money and chatting about other light hearted things purposely to forget about the conversation. However, after shutting the door behind her, Macon placed her hand directly on the area where she was kicked and rubbed the sore spot. It was real. The whole encounter was real, but instead of trying to prove it, she remained silent, speaking no more about it to Braille and never admitting the entire story to Greg. Things were going too perfect to allow old country tales and superstition to spoil the rest of the night, including the hopeful future. The secret would be held close to her heart and considered a fluke.

||

"How was work? You look extra tired, baby." She took his lunch bag from his hand and went to take his plate from the oven. She'd kept it warm for him using an aluminum pie pan. For dinner, she'd cooked some candied yams, pork chops, collard greens and biscuits with rice, enough to last two days. Normally, she didn't cook so much, but with the amount of constant worrying she did all day about Sunni, she remained in the hot kitchen to keep her mind occupied.

"Hey, didn't you forget something?" he asked, following her into what felt like a fiery furnace. There was never any amount of cool air coming from a fan or the brand new air conditioning wall unit that could cool off the kitchen whenever the oven was turned on. It would always feel like a boiler room, and Greg hated to see his beautiful wife trying to hide her sweat and look flawless for him. He would see the passion she put in to making the evening calm and relaxing for the family, and he appreciated it while, at the same time, wishing it was easier on her.

"What did I forget? Oh, I did, didn't I?" she smiled as she met him in the middle of the kitchen floor. Lifting her hand to her face, she was about to wipe the sweat about to fall from her forehead, however, before she could, he reached up and did it for her. Then, he took her by the hand to lead her to the living room. There were some pillows on the chair that he used to prop up her feet. It was only then that he gave her a passionate kiss right by the fan.

"See this. This is how I really want you to be."

"Like this?"

"Yeah like this. What's wrong with this?" he asked, shrugging his shoulders and giving her another kiss, this time on her neck. "I don't want you to have to sweat anymore in that kitchen. I know how much you try, and I know this because I used to watch my own mother work inside the house and out. Nobody ever fixed her food for her, you know, fixed her plate. So allow me to do that for you today? How about that?"

"Well, you know I don't normally eat until I clean up …"

"I can do that, too. Besides," he stated, rising from his kneeled position on the floor to sit next to her on the sofa. "I got something for you out there."

Macon couldn't believe what just hit her ears, and it took her no time to jump up from the chair, her hands covering her mouth as she stood there stunned. Greg laughed so hard at her expression until his stomach hurt. "Well, aren't you gonna go out there and see it? Don't just stand there."

Her hands lowered. "Today? You got me a car today? But we just talked about it and…"

"Well, we live here once, don't we? Isn't that what you've been saying lately? I can't be broker than what I am right now twice, now can I? I love you, Macon."

She finally screamed and ran outside. Before she even slipped on her slippers, Sunni ran down the hallway having awakened from her nap as a result of all the noise. When her dad noticed her, he quickly stood and called her over to him where he gave her one quick lift as they followed Macon toward the screen door.

"What's wrong with Mama?"

"Nothing, baby. Nothing. She's just crazy is all. Running outside like she got no sense. The neighbors are gonna wonder what's gotten into her." He walked to the door with his chest full of joy, so much joy, that he decided to send his daughter outside along with her. "Go on. That's you and your Mama's car."

"That's my car?"

"Yeah. That's the car that you're gonna ride in."

Sunni burst through the screen door and joined her mother at the light yellow, two door car which looked like he'd just drove it off of a lot brand new. There were no dents or scratches on it like the other car that sat in the driveway, and when the engine sounded, it was the perfect hum. Even the neighbors came outside to see the new car that was parked in the yard, but Greg stayed inside being the modest person that he was, never wanting to attract too much attention except from those closest to him. Despite the fact that he hid away from the onlookers who were just as excited as Macon and Sunni, he was bound to get the unwanted attention due to the fact that he was the only one on the street, or really the whole block, who owned two whole cars. Now, there were some people who owned a car and a possible, such as a car with a top half and no bottom half or either extra wheels with nothing to which the wheels could hook. It was only the McKinseys who had a full, extra automobile, and it made them the talk of the entire neighborhood.

"Greg, get out here, man!"

"What's that, Tank?" he answered the approaching neighbor who wore a huge grin, impressed by the new car he saw in the yard.

"*What's that*? What you mean, what's that? That car, man. It's a fine one." Tank was Greg's neighbor from two houses down, and although he had a well built house, he mostly lived on the front porch. Many wondered why he just didn't rent out the rest of his house because he was never inside it. He ate and slept on the side of his own house when he thought no one was aware. Tank wasn't always like that, however. His child died in the house. He just dropped dead one day, and there were many nights that Tank couldn't stand being in the house alone. His wife was killed in a civil rights protest leaving him to raise the boy. He never talked about it. He only smiled like nothing was ever wrong. The porch told it all though.

"I bring home what I can, when it's needed," Greg responded taking a deep breath. "This car didn't come easy though. It's an extra payment that I don't know if I need right now. I had plans, but my lady over there has plans, too, so I can't be selfish and just make her focus on mine only. She deserves it. She wants to get back out there since caring for Sunni, I suppose, and get her mind on new things. Different than when we grew up when moms stayed home."

"Well, if you ever need someone to drive it, I'm right down the road."

Greg laughed and watched as Tank mosied over to the car where he laughed a bit with Macon, took his finger across the car's hood, and then placed that same finger on his tongue before snapping his fingers together. At that, Greg backed away from the door, reached inside his pocket and retrieved his wallet. Besides his paycheck which would be given to him the next day, the money in his wallet was all he had besides the one thousand dollars left over in the bank from putting down most of the cash he had for the car to get his payments to an affordable rate. It was most of the savings he'd put away, but he decided to trust in the future this time, something he'd long lost hope in delivering more good than bad.

As a matter of fact, just as Macon expected, it wasn't many days after buying the car that a couple jobs were calling her for interviews, and it made Greg feel even better to know he was able to provide what was necessary once again despite all odds. A week after he brought the car home, she was already dropping Sunni off with Braille, and sometimes taking Sunni with her on job interviews. It was on a particular Friday that Macon was called for the best interview yet, working at the grocery store downtown which would allow her to get off in just enough time to get home for Sunni when she started school and get dinner done for the family before bedtime.

"So, I see you have work experience, but you haven't worked in a while. Why is that?"

"I've been at home, raising my child until she starts school. My plan is to start working as soon as possible once school starts."

"Not before? We have the position available in three weeks. School doesn't start in at least four."

"Four would be what I need," she stated before figuring out that she was going to have to sell herself due to the time inconvenience. "You only have to teach me something once, and I'll remember it like you taught me twice. I'm just that sharp. If you wait for me for just one extra week, I'll give you a week for half the pay. I really need this job." Macon, concerned about all the money her husband gave up just to support her desires, continued to think up everything she needed to say just to get the job.

The interviewer stood up from her desk, showcasing her gray below the knee skirt and professionally tucked white blouse, without uttering another word which caused Macon to become slightly nervous as she watched the woman walk towards the office door. Macon twisted around in her chair, desperately wanting to hear a positive answer. Instead, she heard...

"Follow me, please. I would like to show you around, just to make certain that this is a job you can handle. It requires you to be here at eight o'clock. It's not a full eight hours, and sometimes, we have to cut back, but seeing as though you already have prior obligations with your child, you won't be the one begging for more hours to work, now will you?"

"So, does that mean I have the job?"

The woman's glasses dropped to her nose and glanced over Macon's long sky blue dress that covered everything except her long, brown arms and flawlessly painted, red fingernails while her hair remained pulled back in a tight bun at the back of her head to reveal the entire shape of her oblong face and high cheekbones. Macon felt uneasy with the way the woman shifted her eyes across her make, but when she spoke, a sigh of relief came forth from her chest.

"So far you do," the woman stated with a small smirk. "As long as the boss says yes to what I have to tell him about you, then yes it will be." Then, she loosened up and whispered, "I think I can sell him on the four weeks you need to wait. And don't concern yourself with my cold nature. It's just for the job." She quickly wiped the smile from her face and gestured for Macon to come forward and keep the pace up so that it would appear that she was working hard when in reality she was hardly working. Macon didn't know what to do with all the chatter she was being given. She didn't know whether to laugh with the woman or remain silent for fear it was all a set up, a test to see if she was serious enough for the job. Instead of doing either, she decided to smile without showing any teeth and nod. That way, she could make the excuse that she was nodding and smiling because she was listening, and if she needed to, she could also say she was laughing along. Either way, it would work in her favor, and obviously it did because it wasn't one full tour around the store and a whole thirty minute wait on the boss that landed her the job. She would start in four weeks, and the pay was good at one dollar and seventy-five cents an hour.

She pulled up to her front yard with tears in her eyes from all the yelling and praising God she did on the way back home. Instead of going to Braille's house to pick up Sunni, she rushed into her own house to start preparing dinner. That way, she could leave the meatloaf in the oven already cooking in order to have the food ready ahead of schedule.

"I got the job! I got the job," she sang, dropping her clothes onto the bed and running back up to the kitchen with only her cream slip on and matching brazier. "Thank you, Jesus, I got the job. That's the most I have ever been paid. Ever. Oh, God, thank you that you always know what we need, and you are *always* on time."

She danced around in her kitchen while singing a sweet song and preparing the ground beef for the meatloaf, cracking some eggs along with some onions and other seasoning to put inside it. As she mixed the ingredients together with her bare hands, the smile never disappeared from her face. Finally, she retrieved the loaf pan from the cabinet and stuffed the raw meat inside then shoved it into the oven.

She hadn't skipped since she was a child, but skipping was exactly what she did on the way back to her bedroom where she removed her hair from the tight bun and allowed her hair to fall wildly. With a small brush, she bumped the ends of her hair into a higher curl so that it wouldn't drape onto her shoulders. From there, she fixed her make-up, slid on a one piece and headed out the door, anxious about sharing the good news. It took her less than five minutes to get to Braille's house, and when she parked, in five seconds she was at the front door, banging on it like a child that has to use the bathroom.

"Braille! Braille," she called, "Open up. It's me, Macon." Usually on a hot day like this, she would have been able to see straight into the house because only the screen door would be used to circulate any scarce amount of cool air through the home. This particular day, the main door was shut, and after Macon pressed her ear up against the door to receive no signs of Sunni nor Braille inside, she began to search the compact yard area. "Braille?" she called again. "Sunni!"

Stepping from the front of the house and toward the room windows at the front and side of the small home, there was no noise or anything else that would alert her to them being home. She began to assume they went for a walk, however, as she approached the back of the home, she saw them walking back toward the house from the wooded area a short distance from Braille's yard. At first, she smiled at the sight of the two, however, the closer they got, her smile faded away, and she began to run. She ran as fast as she could run, not yelling a word as she struggled to keep her emotions together. She heard Braille saying something, but she couldn't understand a word because she was focused so intently on Sunni who walked along side Braille like everything was okay. The problem was that she didn't appear fine. She looked like she had been hurt, and the closer she got, it looked like she was covered in mud and blood.

Falling to her knees once she was able to reach out and touch her daughter's hand, Macon rubbed her all over her dirty clothing and splotches of red on various parts of her legs and shoes. "What happened to you?" Sunni didn't respond, so Macon then turned to Braille who stood tall but without her normal confidence. "Braille? What were you and Sunni doing back there in the woods?"

"She left the yard," Braille stammered, uneasy with a paranoid tension she felt all around her, like there was another ominous presence there that she couldn't see.

"That's it? She left the yard? How did she get like this?" Macon asked, wiping Sunni who stood there blank faced, as if she was in another world. "Sunni, Sunni?" She shook her daughter until she snapped out of her unusual daze. "What happened to you? How did you mess up your clothes? What is all this?" she asked, wiping a red substance from her skin and clothing. "Is this blood?"

Finally, Braille interjected, "When I went to the bathroom, I'd let her play where she was, outside like normal, Macon, but when I came back out, she was gone. You know I let her play out back all the time," she responded, cautiously looking down at her little cousin and then back into the woods quickly.

"Yeah, yeah, I know you do, so Sunni, why did you run back into the woods? You know better!"

"I looked everywhere for her, and then I called her but got no answer. That's when I ran into the woods. That was the only place I didn't check," she continued out of breath but shifting her eyes to the ground, afraid to look into Macon's face. Macon noticed her cousin's hesitation and how she stood a larger distance from Sunni than normal. Most of the time, the two fit together like glue. This time, Braille stood with a noticeable gap, prompting Macon to stand squarely in front of her and repeat herself, sterner than before.

"Braille, I'm not a dummy. What happened in there?" she asked, lifting her arm to point into the woods. "Answer me!" she shouted, but when Braille didn't answer, she warned, "If you don't tell me, I'm going to find out myself!" Assuming the worst of all worsts, she marched toward the woods like a soldier ready to fight any and everything that could have hurt her daughter, unwilling to let the situation pass until she got answers.

"Macon!" Braille called fearfully after her before she was able to enter the woods. "Macon, just stop!" she yelled to no avail. She, then, turned her attention to Sunni who just stood there watching her mother, and the closer she looked, she became very disturbed by a small, demented smile creeping across the muddied child's face. Suddenly, Braille's horrified gaze was broken when Sunni shouted for her mother.

"Mom, I fell down. That's all. I just fell. It was some sap and mud all everywhere," she paused as if she was getting instruction from within the air before continuing to speak, "and some red berries, too," she added as Braille stood in terror at what she was seeing, but she failed to respond in reprimand like she normally would have. The situation had her frozen in fear.

Macon stopped in her tracks, but kept her eyes at the woods, scanning for anything that made sense, anything that corresponded to the confusion she felt. She was only a foot or two away from entering the blanket of trees when a strong sense that something was very much wrong took over her inner being. She needed to find out if it was just all in her mind or if there was something else out there that harmed her child.

"Mama, come on!" Sunni called again.

Startled and with tears of rage streaming down her face as she thought about all the sinister things that could have potentially happened to her daughter in the darkness of the trees, she finally stormed back toward them both as they stood watching her. Macon's eyes were dead set on Sunni, and there wasn't a smile on her face. When she was toe to toe with Sunni, she angrily grabbed her by the wrist and shot a glance a Braille that cut her soul deeply, however, Braille remained silent.

"Let's go." She yanked her daughter forward, turning away from Braille, leaving her standing there in the middle of the grass alone. It was rare to see Braille as frightened as she was because there was hardly anything that ever scared her. Besides her fear, she knew that Macon suspected something was wrong, horribly wrong, but she didn't have the courage to speak up and tell her. Instead, she just stood there until she could see them no more as they walked to the front of the house. Then, she faced the trees once more before running her fastest until she reached the safety of her home.

Searching and dumping through everything she had in her polished, yet old and broken down, dresser, she looked for the items that her mother passed down to her which were passed down to her mother long before she died. She hadn't even so much as seen the items in years, so she hoped that she hadn't hidden them from herself in her comings, goings and cleanings. It was when she felt beneath her dresser that she found exactly what she needed.

It was a flat box made of run down cardboard. The sides of the cardboard were taped on all sides except for one. It was this side that opened to reveal the contents of the box. There was also a makeshift handle on it, much like one of a briefcase, but it was hanging on by old tape.

On the outside of the box were the words, *To my daughter Braille.* When she read the words, she felt like her mother was leaning over her, beckoning for her to hurry and reach in. Therefore, she did just that. There were some old raggedy items that she'd gotten from a witch doctor from her country back in Africa. The man gave it to her in order to ward off the demons that lurk and like to hide right in your face. Sure, Braille liked to say she was a Christian, but she'd also never forgotten what her mother told her to keep on hand just in case. This was the first time that she'd felt torn between both beliefs, and she didn't know what to do.

She pulled what looked like a braided bunch of twigs and ashes out of the bag. There were instructions to sprinkle and blow the ashes out in the air and wave the twigs, so that was what Braille did. Her mom had always told her that in this life, there would be things that she would never believe unless she saw them with her own two eyes, and one of those things were bewitched children. The saying was that all of them were out to get anyone around them in order to gain rule over the area and the people.

"I can't believe I got to do this, Mama," she stated as if her mother was there with her as she tossed the ashes and shook the twigs, out of breath from moving so swiftly around the house in a panic. "Sometimes, I thought you were full of fairy tales. I thought that was some old African folklore, but I saw it. I saw it for myself, Ma. It's Sunni. Sunni…of all people," she stressed. "This stuff better work, too, Mama. It better. Everything I know better work, but it don't look like nothing but the same dirt from outside. I know you wouldn't lie to me, Mama, would you? I got to clean up this mess."

She ran to the front door and locked it. Then she unlocked it again just to lock it once more. From there she looked out the window and wept as she recalled exactly what she saw in the woods. She saw her little cousin, but on the inside, it wasn't the same little girl that she knew.

Braille, under so much emotional pressure, squeezed her head and yanked her medium sized afro down to her cheeks, trying to erase the memory of Sunni in those woods, but it kept replaying and replaying until she finally had to drop the voodoo ashes. "Mama, this ain't nothing but dirt!" she screamed before dropping to her knees to pray. "Please, protect Macon from that girl. She ain't right. She just ain't. She gonna do something bad to my cousin. I know she will, Jesus. I can't let that happen, and Lord, You can't let that happen. I love Macon. She all I ever had. You know I can't think straight all the time, so I can't pray straight either, so please figure it out for me. Just figure it out." She fell asleep at the door repeating the same prayer, frightened with a devastated heart. Meanwhile, Macon proceeded in her line of questioning for Sunni.

"Now you look here, Sunni," she commanded, elevating her voice as she removed her daughter's clothing, "Tell me the truth. I won't be mad."

"You already are."

"No I'm not. I'm concerned about you. I'm frustrated about seeing you covered in only God knows what and your cousin behaving as if she is afraid to tell me what really happened. Now you tell me, because there is nothing, and I mean nothing, to be afraid of right now, see." She turned Sunni's body around to prove that no one was around in the home but them. "Now," she sighed, attempting to relax in order to digest whatever Sunni says. "I want to know."

"I went into the woods."

"What happened in there, and why did you go, honey?" she asked, fighting to camouflage her anxiety and anger.

"I wanted to go in there because I thought I saw something."

"It's dangerous in there."

"It's not. It's just trees."

"It's dark and …"

"I'm not afraid of the dark. It gets dark in here at night. Does that mean it's dangerous in here at night? Could it be dangerous in here at night in the dark?"

Sunni's line of questioning caused Macon to eerily stare at her daughter, not understanding why the questions she asked her prompted so many strange questions and analogies back. "Sunni, it's not the same thing. We are here with you in *this dark*, in this house. You are alone in the woods, in *that dark*. Do you understand? Now stop questioning me, and answer what I ask. What happened in the woods?"

"Are you getting mad, Mama?"

"Just answer me!" she yelled, having grown impatient.

"I told you," she calmly stated before repeating herself, this time with a stream of tears coming down her face. "I already told you."

"Tell me again," Macon ordered as her temperature rose as a result of her own furor. She began to breathe deeply, but the meditation was barely working.

There was silence as Macon looked into her daughter's gorgeous, dark brown eyes. She had the biggest eyes of all the babies in the nursery when she was born, and her tears were always the saddest tears her mom had ever laid eyes on. However, as she waited on an answer to come through those same sad tears, she got an answer she didn't expect.

Sunni wiped the tears from her eyes until there were no signs of sadness left. Then, she spoke clearly, as if she was never upset. "No."

"No? Are you disrespecting me?" When she got no answer, she grabbed the little girl's arm and repeated herself, hoping that the force shook some sense into her so there would be no added consequences to her rebellion. "Are you? Are you back talking me?"

"Are you gonna beat me until you see blood come out…just like the blood you pretended not to see on my clothes and on my skin?" she asked her mother firmly yet softly, as if she'd already rationalized her response. Her voice wasn't childlike and timid, but sure and almost mocking, and as Macon crouched there, feeling miles away from Sunni, she didn't even hear husband's car pull into the driveway. She knelt there, mesmerized and confused, only snapping out of her daze when when Sunni took off down the hall wearing only her undergarments to greet her dad as he came through the door.

"Daddy!"

Macon's attention dropped down to the soiled clothing she'd removed from Sunni. Then, she picked them back up. She'd worn a light blue shirt with frilly short sleeves that cut off just below the shoulder, and the shorts were tan, some old ones that she'd kept in good condition, so much so that they looked nearly as new as the day she bought them. Even her well worn, slide-in outdoor shoes were painted with stains that can't be kicked up from just walking or running in the grass or on concrete, even in the woods on branches and sticks. The stains were as clear as the summer day. She lifted her fingers slowly and wiped across the mud, her fingers quivering like they would on a freezing, winter night. As her fingers reminded her of each texture and what it was, her fingertip finally reached the red. There was blood, fresh blood, barely smeared on her fingers. Sunni's confessed words screamed in her ears as if she stood right beside her, and she immediately dropped the shoe, lost in whatever story was being hidden by both Braille and Sunni. However, something still wasn't right. Sunni had no cuts anywhere on her body.

There wasn't one scar or scratch, not a bruise or hint of one.

Nevertheless, she quickly tossed the clothes away, shoving them underneath the pile of dirty clothes in the hamper, and shook off her raw, warring emotions. Then, she stood strong and walked into the hallway, silently coaching herself to forget about it – for now – until she had a full and complete story. There was too much at stake when it came to Greg, his potential mental relapse of hearing such news, and how he felt about Sunni's safety.

"Hey, sweetheart. Where are you clothes?"

Although Greg was speaking to Sunni, Macon checked her own clothing and hair to make certain they both looked reasonably neat. She hadn't seen herself since she ran out toward the woods to get Sunni, and she didn't even know if any of the stains had gotten on her house dress. She quickly searched her dress one last time but saw nothing. Then, she took her fingers and lightly patted her face before she tuned in to their conversation once more. Sunni sounded like herself again, an innocent, little girl, very different than the daughter who spoke to her seconds ago, filled with an unfamiliar assertion not normal for a girl her age. Not normal for Sunni.

"They got dirty today at cousin Braille's. I took 'em off."

"Go on, now, and get a bath," he advised. "Looks like you got dirty, too, not just those clothes."

"I am. I was in the dirt."

Those words stung Macon like a knife to the chest after what Sunni had already told her. Her chest felt like boulders weighed it down as she shoved what she knew of the true story back inside her womb, all the way back from where Sunni came. There was no story to talk about to Greg nor anyone else because even she didn't believe every thought racing through her head. Macon suddenly became startled once she heard a call for her.

"Where ya' mama?" he asked, expecting her to come around either corner, from the kitchen or the hallway, at any second. He was accustomed to her kiss as soon as he came in from work, so it was odd that she wasn't ready to kiss him back. That was their greeting each and every day since their engagement…a kiss.

"Back here." Sunni grabbed her dad's hand and leaned forward as he leaned backward in a playful attempt to make her pull harder to get him to walk down the hallway.

"I can't get there, Sunni. You got to pull me. Pull!"

"I'm pulling," she laughed, and as she turned to go down the hallway, Macon stood there swallowing the fact that Sunni lied to her, behaving as if she did nothing wrong…once again. As Greg moved toward her, she forced herself to ignore Sunni's presence as the little girl grazed her thigh playfully. With the memories of how her mother used to always consider peace and strength in the house a must, Macon gained the strength not to mention anything to Greg. It would only cause confusion to disrupt what would have been a normally good day, and she didn't want any of that. Instead, she made an announcement before he kissed her, causing him to stall only centimeters from her lips. The interruption was intentional. Her lips were quivering.

"I got the job."

The news was supposed to be delivered in a way that made her want to jump atop her husband and scream at the top of her lungs, however, it didn't make her want to do such a thing at all. Instead, the words felt like huge block and chain about her throat as the revelation was choked by each one of Sunni's abnormal incidents that she'd hidden from him. Suddenly, as she stood there reminded of how she pushed and provoked Greg to look to a brighter future and buy another car, she felt like she'd made the wrong decisions, from taking a job to even having thoughts that maybe the bad in life had let up. Despite her regrets, however, she remained quiet about the latest revelation in order to keep the home at peace.

"You got the job! That's wonderful, baby. You don't start before Sunni…"

"No, I sure don't," she hesitated, forcing a better mental attitude once she saw the excitement blossom across his weary face, proving that he'd had a rough day. It made her certain that she made the right decision to keep quiet about everything, at least for the moment. "They said they would hold the position for me until she starts school. Can you believe that? The lady in there was so nice. At first, she was stuffy, but I found out quickly that she was just putting on for her boss who said yes to me."

"So you start when Sunni goes to school?"

"Sure do."

"Will you be home before she gets out?"

"Sure will, and they're paying me a good one dollar and seventy-five cents!"

"Maybe we can get some of this money back then, huh?" he laughed, breathing a sigh of relief. "May I get my kiss, please, now, Mrs. McKinsey?"

She leaned in and kissed him on his lips as she noticed little Sunni staring at them from behind. Normally, she would have never noticed a thing, but this time she did, causing her to turn her eyes, move away from Greg, and gently take his lunch from his hand on the way toward the kitchen.

"I need to get to Sunni and that bath…and check this meat."

"Smells like loaf."

"That's because it is," she smiled. Pretending like she was in a rush, she lovingly pushed past him while calling for Sunni to go and wait inside the bathroom. Macon never turned around to see if Sunni was following her instruction. Instead, she listened as Greg walked her into the bathroom and turned on the bath water. He then yelled back to her, "I got it, Macon. You go on and cook!"

"Okay," she whispered, but repeated herself louder as she fidgeted with her hands. "Okay! I hear you!" Immediately, she ran to the phone to dial. "Pick up your phone, Braille. Pick it up." Pacing in a small area of the floor, she awaited an answer to follow the ring, but there wasn't one. She hung up the telephone and called again and then one more time after that, but it was no use. The calls remained unanswered, tempting her to leave the house and drive back over, however, she didn't want to cover a lie with another. Therefore, she calmed herself down and finished dinner, hoping that there would be no more odd incidents from Sunni any longer. There wasn't.

Still yet, she remained bothered for the nights afterwards, fighting with if she should tell Greg and never being able to reach Braille so she could explain the unexplainable. Braille had been avoiding her. There were so many unknowns, so she decided that she would control what she could control and that was how much Greg's knowledge of the situation would be. The nightmares he used to have were some of the most frightening things she'd ever seen. He would wake up apologizing while believing he was holding their deceased baby in his hand. He wouldn't stop apologizing until he fell back to sleep. Sunni was perfect in his eyes, and she couldn't risk him being triggered at the hint that something was wrong with her.

Thankfully, there was nothing that occurred out of the ordinary for weeks, and not only was Sunni on her way to her first day of school for her first day of work, Greg decided to go in to work late in order to see her catch the school bus for the first time and also see Macon off for her first day at the job.

CHAPTER 4

"Bye, honey. Remember to eat all of your lunch, and your teacher's name is Mrs. Jackson. Respect her and do as she says, okay? She's a nice lady," Macon reminded her as she kissed her daughter on the cheeks a multitude of times at the bus stop. Greg then picked her up and kissed her on her forehead before handing her over to one of the older girls whom volunteered to keep her safe on and off the freshly painted bus.

"I will bring her back home with me, Mr. McKinsey."

"You do that for me, you hear? Get a good snack at the house, too, before you go home."

"Okay."

"Bye, Ma. Bye, Daddy!" shouted Sunni as she cheerfully stepped onto the bus wearing her yellow floral dress with brown sandals to match. Her dark brown hair was done in pig tails all around her head and little yellow barrettes that she loved to shake whenever she felt the urge.

As Greg and Macon looked on, they felt relieved that they had someone available with whom Sunni knew and felt comfortable around to keep her safe to and from school. The young girl, Jasmine, who was keeping watch over her, grew up in the neighborhood and had never been in any trouble. She was only nine years old, but she was very responsible for her age and loved watching children. She had a little brother of her own who wasn't quite ready to enroll in school, but she couldn't wait for him to join her on the bus. Therefore, when Macon asked her to keep an eye on Sunni, Jasmine jumped at the chance to take the duty on.

"Looks like Jasmine is just as happy as Sunni."

"It sure does, doesn't it?" Macon responded cheerfully as the bus took off down the road. "I'm gonna miss my baby."

"I already do." Greg continued with nervous banter, holding her hand as they walked back to the house. "It's gonna be alright, Macon, won't it?" he asked, not needing an answer, but instead trying to comfort them both, especially himself, because he felt the will to follow her since it was the first time he'd left her alone with anyone except his wife or Braille. The pain came

81

back of not being there to stop the worse from occurring. Macon felt it in the sweat that poured from his palm.

"Yes…I know it will," she replied, strengthening her answer to bond with him where he was weak, but also needing to release her anxiety with him carefully as well. "I was just thinking about my new job. It's this job and being away from home again. I'm so used to being home and at Sunni's every beck and call. It's not like that anymore. I feel guilty, almost lost, even though it's giving me – us – more freedom." She then whispered as her mind took her back to the incidents that happened a couple weeks ago. "I'd even been wondering if taking this job was actually the right thing to do." Macon knew that it was possibly the wrong thing to say, but she was slightly hoping that Greg would tell her to quit, but then again, also wanting him to encourage her at the same time. She didn't know what reply Greg would give her just as much as she didn't know what she really wanted.

He stopped and stood in front of her. "Now, this was your choice. I done gone and bought that car for you," he smiled, peeking back at the school bus as it turned the corner, "And I expect you need to go somewhere for all the money I spent. You're not staying home, though," he laughed. "No ma'am. Home will be empty for half the day. That car has to leave here!"

"Shut up, Greg. Thank you." She peeked up at him with a grin spreading across her face as they continued walking. "I am excited though. Sunni's gonna be okay. She will be just fine," she continued to convince herself.

‖

Reporting to her first day at work was optimistic. As in the same way she interviewed, she pulled her hair up in a bun and wore comfortable clothes, and as soon as she arrived, she was assigned duties. They gave her a uniform to wear, and it fit perfectly despite her not remembering giving them her size. The uniform for the store was gray and blue while the shoes were required to be black or white. She'd already been told about the shoes, but when she got the uniform, she wished she'd had chosen white shoes.

Her job consisted of arranging the items on the store shelves, assist customers, and whenever that was complete, she was to learn the register. The store was the largest on that side of town, selling mostly groceries with a small corner of the store devoted to crafts and hardware which were items that many people in Oaksprings needed to keep them afloat. There were many seamstresses in town, some of the best. That was why so many people from neighboring cities came to find out who was the best at it. The great thing about Oaksprings County was that it was surrounded by towns that consisted of some of the wealthy and some of the poor. Most people in Oaksprings were earning just enough money to make it out of where they came from, and that place was poverty. They ended up stuck in the middle, like a lower middle class. The wealthy only hired from within Oaksprings, and the poor found work in the same area. Oaksprings was the bridge, linking one city to another, because without it, no one would reach out and touch one another at all.

"New here?"

Macon's attention was captured by a tall, slender, white male who appeared to be in his late twenties. He displayed an openness in the way he carried himself, very upbeat as he whistled, placing a heavy closed box right beside her. She assumed the box was placed there for her to sort things from it, however, he didn't leave her to herself. Instead, he retrieved a box cutter from his pocket and opened the box right there in front of her and began stocking the shelves.

"Did you hear me?" he asked again, flashing a smile. "New here?"

"Oh yes…I thought I did answer you," she laughed quietly. "Maybe not with words, but I nodded."

"Oh, I'm sorry then. I didn't see you. It's a bad habit of mine to not stand at attention and look directly at people when I chat. Most times, I continue doing whatever I'm doing…just like now. I'm James."

Macon hesitated, but then, reached inside the box along with him in order to become more friendly and helpful, pulling out more cans of food. "I'm Macon. It's nice to meet you, James. I'll help you with this."

"Nice to meet you, too. No sense in helping me when they got you doing something else. Never take on someone else's responsibility when yours isn't fully done. That's the first rule I learned at this store."

Macon looked back at her shelf, and he was right. She had to not only organize but place the price tags on each box or can that didn't have one attached. Only half her row was finished.

"The boss is a stickler about that. He loves everything in order. You won't see him mostly though. Instead, you'll see the supervisor who thinks she's the boss half the time. The other half of the time, she thinks she's your friend. She flip flops, so don't trust her. She'll have you axed before she'll take the blame for you so that she can save her job. She actually takes all the so-called work from him which is why she's still working. It leaves him with nothing to do."

Stunned at his admission about those in charge and how freely he revealed the information, she quickly regained her posture where she was working and made a point not to reply or gesture anything that was in agreement with what he stated. This wasn't her first time on a job, and she knew that she couldn't ever trust the one who talked too much. She also knew that no matter how friendly he was, she was still the brownest lady she saw on the floor. That meant that she needed to watch her every word and move, far more than the white young man beside her, although it sounded like he meant no harm to her.

"Are you from Oaksprings orignally?"

"Not originally, no. I'm from CaseTown," she admitted with her head held high as she was already aware of the potential for people to look down on her and others from that area. She was from one of the poorest sections of the small city of CaseTown called Maze. Sometimes, the name would make people who lived there laugh because it was a place that was so hard to get away from, or escape, and that fit the name – Maze. Although all were poor there, they were well raised, everyone in the area, and they simply just wanted a little extra out of life as far as opportunity. Most people out of Maze would prefer to take that section of town with them if they were able to do better because it was honestly an ideal place to grow up and live, but it just needed more finances due to everything breaking down and no one having the funds to fix things back up. The government sure wasn't budgeting out money their way even though taxes were paid on time and by everyone, so the people of Maze were all on their own.

"CaseTown? My wife is from CaseTown."

Macon, being shocked at his words, quickly thought up something to say pertaining to him being married although that wasn't what took her by surprise. "You're married? You look so young."

"Everyone says that. I'm thirty-five."

"I would have never known," she smiled, still reeling from the fact that his wife is from the same city where she was born and raised. She took a closer look at him, noticing the smaller details of his face and frame. After seconds of silence, Macon pushed herself up to ask, "Is your wife…"

"She's my age, well, just two years younger," he interjected quickly although that wasn't what she was going to ask him.

"Well, I was going to ask if she…"

"She's pregnant, too. Well, we…pregnant. You're the first person I've told actually," he interjected. "Some have already seen her," he drifted.

Although continuously interrupted by his unwillingness to let her get her full question out, she responded positively, "Congratulations. I'm honored."

"We just want to know it's going to be safe…even thinking about moving back to CaseTown. She's from the south," he paused, "of the city."

Macon placed the can of beans back on the shelf but held on to it. Then, she turned slowly toward him which brought the glistening of tears to his eyes, and she could tell he harbored troubles in his soul. He glanced back at her, having already willed the forming tears away, before she spoke again very carefully. "I was getting ready to ask you where she went to school and what part of CaseTown she was from because since we are about the same age, I might know her." She looked away. "We could have even gone to the same *schools* at some point," she stated, stressing the word schools being that the educational system was still highly segregated when she was a child, and despite the law, still were. She placed another can on the shelf and then watched him retrieve his empty hand from the box. She noticed it trembling uncontrollably before he shoved it through his short brown hair to hide his anxiety.

"I know what you're asking me. Not too many of my kind in the south of CaseTown, or even in CaseTown at all so…"

Terrified, Macon quickly responded, "No, no, no…I'm just asking if she went to school at…"

"She's…she looks like you," he admitted, referring to the color of his wife's skin, "and she doesn't come outside anymore since the pregnancy. I just needed someone around here to be happy for us instead of terrified of supporting or just not gawking at us when we sneak out together, even in the yard. You're the first person who came from her area in a long time to work here. Most folks that know of me and my wife's situation won't accept us together…separately but not together. I don't know what they will do when they find out we're having a baby because that's gonna be us in one body that can't be separated," he smiled. "I hear moving up north won't help much either. We've been threatened…"

Macon fell silent. She knew the implications of having such a relationship and to make matters even more complicated, having a child in a union like that. Many people of his kind just didn't care for it, but it seemed that it faired only slightly better somehow when a white man was with a black woman and not vice versa. There was for sure trouble if a black man was with a white woman every time. The whites couldn't stomach it, and they would voice their disapproval every second they could. It was never safe for a couple bold enough to do it, especially for the one covered in brown skin.

Finally, she spoke up, feeling guilty about not having much to say although she wanted to encourage him. "I understand. Well, maybe I can talk to her some time. Maybe come by and …"

"Yes. You sure can." He quickly pulled out a pencil and scribbled his address and phone number on a sheet of paper and handed it to her. Macon, seeing the urgency, took it and slid it into her pocket. From there, the conversation grew silent, and they continued working as if nothing occurred. Even conversations about blacks and whites marrying or being married in the deeply, isolated south wasn't received with open arms. Although desegregation already passed years prior, the hearts of racism had no law. It felt what it felt unless they gave it up to God's true way. By the end of Macon's shift, she was relieved to get home and wait for her daughter to arrive at the bus stop.

"I only have five minutes. Hurry up, Macon, hurry up," she pressured herself as she ran back up the hallway after changing clothes. "Don't miss this one. Don't you dare miss this one," she smiled, awaiting the second she would get to hear all about Sunni's first day in school. She was out of the front door in no time, and by the time she got to the bus stop, she heard it pulling around the corner. There it was rolling towards her, and her heart was all but too ready to reunite with her kindergartener.

"Macon. Macon!" a voice called from behind causing her to turn and face the person whom she hadn't spoken to in weeks. Every time Macon called her on the phone to clarify what happened to Sunni, there was no answer, and when she went by the house, there was also no answer. However, this afternoon, of all afternoons, the person whom she figured would appear whenever she was ready to do so was standing behind her at the school bus stop. It was obvious why she was there, or so Macon thought.

"Braille?"

"Leave that girl on the school bus." Braille exhaled heavily, like something had been plaguing her for a while. Although she had lost weight a while back for her stay in the hospital, she was visibly much smaller than the day she was released, even to the point where she looked sick again. Her weight loss was far faster than anything considered normal which prompted Macon to rush to her, no longer upset with her close cousin but concerned that she wasn't fully healed from the pneumonia when she left the hospital.

"Braille? What's wrong?" she asked, examining her frail body, totally not aware of what Braille stated on the way up the sidewalk.

"You gotta let her stay on that bus."

"What?" Macon retorted, quickly realizing that Braille's being there wasn't a cordial stop.

"Leave her…just leave her. Come on." She reached to tug at Macon, but Braille's efforts to pull her were stopped with a firm smack to her wrist.

"Get your hands off of me, Braille. Are you crazy? Huh?" she shouted, pulling away while looking back, embarrassed at her cousin's actions as the school bus van approached to a standstill. "You can't drag me away from my own child! What's wrong with you? Are you going crazy?" She stared her cousin over like there was more than her weight that she was losing because she was behaving like she was losing her mind.

"You can pull away from me if you want to, but I know what's going on. You didn't see it!" Braille's eyes were flushed red, like she hadn't slept for days on end while her skin was dry through to every layer. If no one knew it, they would believe that she was caught up in the bad times of life and sleeping on the streets.

"See what? What didn't I see? And calm down!" Macon fired off, glancing around their space to see if anyone was watching. "I've been trying to talk to you about it because…"

"You didn't see it! And I'm telling you because I love you, and you're all I got left. We made a promise to each other," she stated, fighting back the streaming evidence of a heart full of turmoil. "That child ain't right. Sunni ain't right, and she ain't never gonna be right. Her ailment is down to the root, and it needs to be chopped off. I know it's gonna be hard because all these days it was hard for me to do it, but I did it. Some of them like that have to be cut off from the rest, and you know that!"

Macon immediately became enraged at the notion that Braille thought Sunni should be abandoned and left to just die. That was what she meant by chopping her off. The old folks used the phrase a lot when she was growing up, but no one ever did anything close to it except for those who had strict ties to the old way, found in beliefs that originate in some parts from Africa.

"You shut up and leave! Yeah, we made a promise that nobody would ever separate us, but that never included me putting anyone over my own daughter. You need help putting things in perspective, Braille. You always have," she scowled, canvassing their immediate area to detect anyone walking to closely to them in order to gather the substance of their conversation. "Don't you ever…" she started as the bus driver got out to help the children exit.

"She was digging out the blood!" She threw her fists down by her sides like she was attacking the air she breathed while sealing her eyes closed so tightly that the wrinkles on her eyelids shown distinctly. "I didn't want to believe it, so I lied. I lied, I lied and kept quiet," she shook with grief, wounds of a struggle apparent as she wrestled to keep her voice down. "I was so scared, but Sunni…she was playing in it and smiling about it. She killed it herself! I'm warning you. My mama told me about the cursed child, and she is one. It's true. It's all true," she continued through the quivering of her voice while closing the distance between herself and Macon. "Just as soon as you close your eyes, that girl will bring *death*. She's gonna bring death to your front porch." Before Macon could say another word, she noticed the bus driver standing there in awe of what was just spoken about a child on the bus, but he immediately turned away, pretending to have heard nothing. He was an older man, but it was obvious that he heard every word because when Sunni got off the bus with Jasmine, he didn't take his eyes off of her. By the time Macon turned back around to face Braille, she had already walked away at the sight of Sunni, bolting all the way down the sidewalk.

"Where's Auntie Braille going, Ma?" Sunni asked, tugging at her mother's clothing. "Auntie Braille! It was my first day of school today!" she called, but Macon distracted her.

"Hey, baby. Come on. Let's go home. Braille just brought me something. She had to run along, but she told me to tell you that…she is proud of you."

"What did she bring you?"

"Nothing that you can see with your eyes, Sunni." She reached down and picked her up while nodding to Jasmine. "Thank you, honey. Come on by and get something to eat…a snack, okay? Ask your Mom first, alright? I got her from here. Hurry up now," she smiled, needing to come through on the promise Greg made Jasmine about giving her a snack as a thank you for taking care of Sunni.

"Yes ma'am. I will. She was good, too."

"You were?"she stated, admiring Sunni, however, fighting with Braille's words mentally.

"Yep, and school was fun. We got to play, and there were a bunch of other children there with me, like you and daddy said."

"I know. I told you. Some even from this neighborhood."

"Even on the bus with me!"

"Yes ma'am," Macon nodded.

"I go back tomorrow right?"

"Sure you do, but right now, focus on telling me what you brought home, just tell me everything about your day, while I cook you and your father a nice meal before he gets home." While they walk down the road, Macon had already determined that she would see Braille that night after she tucked Sunni into bed. The chirp of Sunni's voice soothed her worries slightly as she continued to rub Sunni's small hand in between her own nervously, until she opened the door of her home and began to unload her cares into passionately caring for her family in a home cooked meal.

"I need to go to Braille's tonight. She needs my help with something." Greg knew nothing about the awkward silence them that has lasted for days nor did he know about the tiff at the bus stop.

"It's getting late, Macon," he complained. "Why you feel like you need to go back out for Braille. Can't it wait until tomorrow?"

"No, it can't wait. She was sick remember? Not only that, I saw her, and she might be relapsing so I need to check on her. Maybe put her some soup on the stove. I'll be back." She slid on her shoes and grabbed her car keys.

"Hurry back, baby. I never have liked you out in the night without me."

"Yeah, I will." She reassured him with a smile and kiss to his lips. "Her number is right there where I leave all of them. If you need to call me, just call me over there, okay? I won't be long. Just check on Sunni while she sleeps. Don't assume she's okay like you always do," she added.

"I always do check on her," he grinned, realizing that he truly doesn't. "Trust me sometimes."

"Alright. I trust you." She rushed away with her hand in the air waving as if everything was fine, but things weren't fine. They were far from fine.

As she rode the short distance to Braille's home, the words she spoke echoed in the same unbearable tone as they had since she left the bus stop. *She killed it.* She recalled the brownish red stains all over her clothing that was explained as sap and mud, but this new story coming from Braille just verified what Sunni stated that particular afternoon right before her daddy got home from work. It was blood.

Imagining that Sunni had actually killed something was too much for her to believe, so no matter what, she was determined to approach Braille about all those mixed up stories and lies that only God knows which to believe, even if it meant losing her as a cousin for the rest of her life. One thing was certain though, no matter how tight their bond, there was no way she was doing what Braille asked of her. She would never leave Sunni, and understanding that would be difficult for Braille due to a slight imbalance that makes her rational thinking become irrational when she is placed under stress. She couldn't allow Braille to lose control and bruise her innocent child's name over foolishness.

She pulled up to the curb, exited the car and slammed the door so hard that she knew beyond a shadow of a doubt that Braille heard her through the thin walls of the small home. "She's home. I know she's home, and she better open this door this time or I'm gonna knock it down myself. Got people staring at Sunni at the bus stop like something is wrong with her," she vented.

There were many people around who grew up like Braille, clinging to superstitions and omens, myths and tales of their late ancestors. Those beliefs all ended for Macon when her mother ended them, teaching her that there was no such thing as trusting in Jesus and hocus pocus. That would be like worshiping God and the devil at the same time, playing by both of their rules, and God doesn't share the throne. Unfortunately, Braille's mother didn't follow suit. She trusted in both, thus continuing to teach it to Braille. When Braille came to the bus stop, Macon knew she was taking her fears back to those old time beliefs. Therefore, she just held all her furor and concern back until the perfect time – when she could confront Braille in private.

She banged on the door like a mad woman, yelling for Braille to open the door, but before the second barrage of bangs, the door flew open to a weeping Braille who was a nervous wreck. That didn't faze Macon at all as she invited herself in to confront her about the fiasco she pulled in front of everyone outside.

"How dare you come to my child's bus stop and tell me to abandon her! Let me tell you something," she warned with her finger headed straight for Braille's head, but Braille moved herself, slapping Macon's finger down. That didn't prevent Macon for shouting on. "You better get yourself together! If you ever harm me or my child with your filthy words again, Braille, I swear I'll fight you myself, and even if I lose, it will be the hardest fight you ever had in your life, and you'll have all the scars to prove it."

"It was Pumpkin!" Braille shouted, having already turned from Macon's fiery words to face the wall. As her back faced a stunned Macon, she continued, bracing herself against the wall with her forehead, rolling it from side to side, toiling with a memory that haunted her each day since its conception. "It was Pumpkin. She killed Pumpkin. At first, I didn't want to believe it…tried to believe it wasn't him what I saw beneath her bleeding to death, but when I put more food out back, he didn't come back to eat like he always does. The food is still out there," she cried. "It's still there. I watched over it every night, stood guard over it so no other animal would get it, until I decided to believe what I saw for good."

Macon backed away from Braille until there was no more room for her to move. Her back hit the wall. Pumpkin was Braille's rabbit, the rabbit that she'd cared for a long time, feeding it whenever she saw it until it made Braille's home its home. Each time Macon came over, there was Pumpkin, and apparently, the rabbit didn't go anywhere when Braille was hospitalized due to the fact that she always kept something outside for the little bunny. There was even a little nest she'd made for him which he learned to sit in once in while, especially if he wanted more to eat or some play time.

"Say something now, Macon, huh? Braille retorted, cocking her head down and to the side in order to see Macon from the side of her eye being held down with silence. "It was your daughter who killed my Pumpkin. I don't have any children, and that rabbit was my child," she cried. Finally, she turned all the way around. "That same Pumpkin that she played with and fed every single time she came over here, she killed. Stabbed and beat him to death. I was scared. I didn't really know what to do or say. I loved them both, but one scares me blind, Macon. One scares me 'til I'm sick."

"What do you mean she killed it? It had to be an accident," Macon whispered, her eyes shuffling, needing to find something around to disprove everything being stated.

"It wasn't no accident!" Braille shouted with her arms and fingers outstretched, pleading with Macon to believe her. "I was using the bathroom. Left her out there like I do sometimes for a minute or two. My flow had come on, so it took longer than usual because I had to change. She was feeding him, like I let her do all the time. I wasn't gone for five minutes, at the most six, and when I called for her, she didn't answer. That's when I got scared because she always answers."

Macon followed the tears streaming down Braille's face, and she knew there was no level of comfort that could have stopped it. Braille was passionate about just about everything, so whenever she cried, she wailed. The same was true about all the other emotions when it came to her. She was double for each dose.

"I didn't know where she was. I was looking all around when I got back out back, but she wasn't answering. I ran out front, and she wasn't there. But when I didn't see Pumpkin after going around back, I figured she could have

followed him. He had a habit of going back and
forth between my house and them woods back
there, so I ran. Kept calling for her, but I ran as
fast as I could. I was scared, Macon, that
somebody took her. She wasn't there," Braille
trembled into a frightened whisper, "But then I
finally saw her."

||

"Eat this, Pumpkin. Here. Eat it." She
glanced behind her and noticed that big cousin
Braille was nowhere in sight. "Come on. Lemme
hold you for a minute, and you eat this while
you're in my arms like a baby. Let's go for a
walk. I gotta hold you tight so don't fight. You're
squishy. You've always been squishy," she
stated, holding Pumpkin at the loose collar made
for him by Braille.

There were some woods located a close
distance to the house, so that was where Sunni
decided to go. Instead of walking, however, she
skipped, and after skipping for a short distance
she turned back, noticing that her cousin had not
returned to the back door. It was then that she
began to run. She ran until she couldn't see the
house anymore, and no one could see her.

"This is where you come from, little Pumpkin?" Unafraid, she searched between the trees for a place to sit, and that was when she heard a voice calling her name. Instead of answering, she found the perfect spot to hide so that she would go unnoticed. On the ground to her side were large rocks and sticks. She took the largest rock that she could hold in her hand as she squeezed the small bunny in her other arm. "I told you that you were squishy. You feel just like my stuffed toys at the house, but you're not. You're alive. But watch me make you like one of my toys, little Pumpkin. You won't move no more. Watch." Then she whispered, as if there was someone standing there playing with her. "Okay…okay…lemme get it."

"Sunni!"

"She's coming!" She glanced up and nodded as she began to bang the head of the little bunny as it struggle to get away, but Sunni leaned atop its body and bludgeoned it repeatedly until it stopped fighting. After the bunny fell limp, she picked up the sticks and began to jab it in every part of its small body. Blood squirt from Pumpkin like water would from a water balloon, getting on her clothes and shoes, and as she continued to stab the motionless bunny, there was Braille standing about five feet away from her, holding her heart like it had already stopped as she waited to fall dead. Sunni had already seen her from the corner of her eye, so she turned slightly so that Braille could see more of her masterpiece. Then, Sunni smiled, continuing her butcher of the pet with whom Braille had fallen so much in love.

"Stop it," Braille uttered as she fell to the ground, holding back vomit and tears once she noticed that the bunny was Pumpkin. Knots twisted up her stomach and her throat quaked with pain as she reached out toward her baby bunny, but Sunni continued to stab it, giggling slightly like she was listening to someone tell a joke, like it was funny to see Braille and the bunny suffer. "I said stop it!" Braille found the strength to stand. "Stop it now!" Braille ordered in a heated rage, storming towards her like she was about to make her suffer the consequences of what she'd done, but before she was able to do anything, she was stopped by Sunni's words.

"This is what's gonna happen to you...*cousin* Braille. Except I'm not gonna do it. He will," she explained, looking over into another part of the woods. Braille lifted her eyes away from the child in a panic, nearly falling over large tree roots in fright, to see what man she was talking about. She lifted her fists to fight, something she'd always had to do so it was like second nature. However, when she saw nor heard anyone there, Sunni giggled again, laughing at Braille's reaction.

"I told you," she whispered, causing Braille attention to fall quickly back on her.

"What did you just say? Who are you talking to?"

Sunni didn't answer as she slowly put the stick down. Pumpkin lay there dead beneath her feet. She stood there for a minute before fearlessly walking out of the woods and towards the house. Braille backed out of the woods, clearly shaken by what she'd seen and heard, continuously checking for anyone tailing them, while not wanting to lay a finger on Sunni.

||

"And that's what happened. I lay my life down right now if that's not the truth. I was scared to tell you. I was terrified, didn't even know how to tell you at the time," she explained, moving morbidly toward Macon who hadn't

108

spoken a word since she began the story. "All I saw was her scooping all the life from my little Pumpkin and then, Macon, when you got here, and she was watching you walk back into the woods," she continued, her voice falling to a frightening whisper, "she smiled. It was a grin like she knew where she was leading you by her lies, manipulating you like she wanted you dead, like she thought it was funny. You her mama, and she was setting you up to die, Macon! She ain't right, Macon. Just like she said some man was gonna kill me, I know she wanted you to die, too. She wanted you to die. She's planning on it, and I don't doubt it's gonna be by her."

"You two told me it was sap and... she told me it was sap one time and blood the next. Which is it? Sap or blood?" Macon ominously retorted in denial of all she was being told. Braille stared back at her in disbelief that she was still questioning the story, especially after hearing that even Sunni told her the truth about the blood. "Where's Pumpkin?" Macon bolted from her position and moved into the backyard where she didn't see the rabbit. "Get a flashlight and take me."

Braille attempted to stop her from going further than the yard. "It's going on nighttime, and she said a man was back there in the …"

"Take me!" she screamed furiously at Braille, angry that the information about Pumpkin wasn't stated weeks ago. "If Pumpkin is dead like you say, take me to him, and I don't care how long it takes to find his carcass. It should still be there…something should. Don't expect me to believe all this without proof, with all these lies…"

Macon was still in denial, so at that, Braille ran back into her bedroom to get her flashlight. She kept two in the house at all times along with the batteries due to the fact that sometimes she wasn't able to pay her light bill and the electricity would be turned off for some days. Braille wouldn't ever tell anyone about it unless the power was shut off in the winter time. If the electricity went out in the summer, she would just turn on her flashlight, eat fruit or nuts, and sit under the shade of the trees in the yard until she could save the money to turn the electricity back on and plug up a fan.

"Here, here," she ran out breathing heavily. "Follow me." Braille toted a bat in her other hand, still suspecting that Sunni knew something that she didn't know about her future demise. She'd grown paranoid since that day, barely able to eat and when she did eat, she couldn't keep anything down. She felt and looked to be wasting away, but before she died or lost her mind, she knew she had to warn Macon. That was what she knew about a cursed child. The belief was that they had a way of either making you feel like you got no hope left until you go crazy or they kill you, and Braille truly felt like she'd been vexed and waiting to die.

"Stay close," she stuttered, "And you keep your light shining that way while I go in the direction of Pumpkin. There's barely any sun left, so it's dark in here. Turn right here, and I'm not going any further, but I'll shine the light. Pumpkin's there. Right there. She had a stick…stabbing him," she cried softly. "There should be a stick there standing upright like I last saw it in Pumpkin's body, if his body is still there."

Macon drifted over toward the area that Braille pointed out, and there a decomposing Pumpkin was. He wasn't jumping around and looking for food like normal. He was dead and had already decomposed to nearly nothing. She knew it was him because of a red rubber band she kept on Pumpkin's foot and a collar that Braille had no intentions of retrieving. Macon immediately fell stomach sick, so she caught hold of a tree right beside her to break the fall that she knew was coming because she'd grown weak in the knees. The flashlight already dropped to the ground.

"Braille," she struggled, "Why didn't you tell me?"

"I couldn't, especially after…"

"You could!" she screamed as she was finally overtaken by the weakness that pulled her to the ground just as simply as raindrops fall from the sky. She had no way to run from her own thoughts as her fears grew beyond what they had in a long time. Finding an escape for Sunni and her recent behavior became more trying, just like keeping it hidden became like a wound that decided never to heal but kept oozing out pus every so often to remind the victim that it needed to be tended to or else. It finally hit her that the worst in life never left. Greg was right. It only waited around to strike again once hope decided to take a stand, once it was easy to box its victim in a corner.

"You let me walk around my own daughter and not once did you tell me she did something like this." Her eyes canvassed the area where Pumpkin's carcass lay, searching for an answer she knew she wouldn't get. "What's wrong with my Sunni, Braille? What's wrong with her? You gotta help me, please."

"Get up. We gotta get out of these woods before it gets too dark. Sunni said somebody told her that he was gonna kill me. She said he was right here in these woods, and I was gonna die just like that so we gotta go. Let's go!"

"Gonna kill you? Ain't a soul gonna kill you! Where are you?" Macon shouted angrily through the leaves, bushes and trees of the blinding forest. "Where are you and leave my daughter alone! Leave my cousin alone! You hear me? Leave us alone."

"Come on, Macon!" She gave Macon the strongest shove she could give her, and she continued shoving her in the back to make her get out of the woods. "Shut up and run. You gonna get both of us killed, now go!"

It wasn't long before they made it back into the house. Braille ran through the home checking every nook and cranny. Macon watched. Everywhere she turned brought back memories of her little girl playing inside Braille's home without incident. Over by the kitchen, she liked to sit and peep through the cracks in the floor, and when she sat at the front door peering out, she would blow her breath on the glass in the winter time to make a misty cloud to write on. Even when Pumpkin came around, she would pet him, feed him. Pumpkin wasn't afraid of her at all.

When Braille briskly walked back by to double check the locks on the door, Macon finally spoke. "How you know she did that all on her own? If a man was there, how do you know he didn't show her how to kill Pumpkin? How do you know he didn't lead her into doing what she did? You weren't watching her the whole time, so how do you know for sure that…"

"I don't. How about that? I don't. All I know is that when I got to her, she was all alone, stabbing my bunny and *enjoying it*. Answer me that. How is it that if a man was there, she wasn't scared? How if a man was there, a strange man, he didn't hurt her, rape her or string her up by some tree after guiding her into the woods instead of showing her how to butcher a bunny? Or how about this…since you still got all the questions, and you out there shoutin' in the woods calling for to meet the strange man who wants to kill me. Are you in on my death along with her? Was that the plan all along, to lead me out there in them sticks to get murdered while you look on and smile?" she asked suspiciously, starting to believe that the trek to the woods and the whole conversation was a big part of the curse's plan being carried out.

"Your death? I love you, Braille, I…"

"I don't wanna hear about no love, Macon! Yes, my death!" Braille then picked up a wooden chair and shoved it up against her back door as she eyed Macon over really hard, harder than what she'd ever done in her whole life. She didn't trust her anymore, especially since it seemed that Macon wasn't convinced yet and still making excuses. "*You* called for him just now, out there in them woods. *You* did," she expressed suspiciously only two or three feet from Macon, causing Macon to become frightened and defensive.

"I don't know any man nor do I even know what you're talking about! I was gonna kill him myself if I had to, and it was you who told me about it. I didn't know anything before I got here

– not one thing. Take your accusations about me somewhere else, and as far as Sunni…"

"There you go again. Sunni is gonna be the death of you, but I ain't gonna sit back and let her kill me, cousin or no cousin." She lunged toward Macon like a woman on the attack, but Macon didn't budge, having already grown so furious at the accusation that she was willing to fight her own cousin. "You mark my words, if there really ain't a man out there waiting to kill us, then Sunni is the one carrying around a dead person inside her already, and it wants us to join in. There are only two options to go with here. Stop being blinded by your love for her. And for most folks around here to think that I'm the one ain't got no sense. It's you! You ain't thinking straight, not me."

Macon lifted her hand to smack Braille in the face, but Braille caught it in mid-air and shoved it down by Macon's side. With sweat pouring down her face and blood shot eyes, she moved nose to nose with her and uttered another warning.

"If you want to do anything for Sunni, you need to get that darkness out of her. Remember what she did to you…outta nowhere? You even told me that yourself." She then let Macon's arm go loose and backed away. "All this ain't a coincidence, a child kicking her own mother in the stomach and acting like it didn't happen and now this. Don't ignore the demons when they introduce themselves loud and clear. Ignoring doesn't make them leave. They just grow, get bigger and larger and wider until…"

"Sunni doesn't have any demons! She's my child!" Macon's voice cut like the sharpest knife as she strained through all of her pain. Then, the small room fell silent, like there was nothing left living and breathing in it. They'd never fought nor had they ever come close, and as they stood there with locked eyes, for the first time they felt like strangers who lived worlds apart. It was all too clear that they were making their best attempt to find each other from within the silence of the living room, but no matter how much they stared at each other, the gulf was wide and deep and at the bottom of that gulf was Sunni and a murdered rabbit that Braille considered as close to a child as she may ever get. There was no bridge.

Finally, Macon softly broke the silence, "I'm sorry about Pumpkin. I know exactly what he meant to you. You should know what Sunni means to me, but for some reason, you don't.

Goodbye, Braille." She turned to leave, refusing
to speak aloud any evil into existence about
Sunni although deep down, she knew she didn't
have to speak it up. It had already invited itself
in.

Braille didn't respond. She'd done all she
could do, and that was too much. However, as
she watched her cousin walk through the front
door, she silently uttered the words with tears
streaming down her dark brown skin, "Don't
go." The door shut softly, her eyes fell to the
emptiness of her home and heart, and she sat on
the floor alone, not caring whether she lived or
died, staring at the front door as it remained
unlocked.

‖

"What's wrong with you, baby?" Greg
asked, having noticed a change in Macon since
she returned home.

"Nothing," she responded while removing
her clothes to get into the bathtub. He entered
the bathroom after her, but she stopped him.
"My flow. It came on."

"Didn't it just…"

"Yeah, but sometimes, it does this. It hasn't come on back to back in a while, many years now, since I had Sunni. It happens. Sometimes nature takes another route like that." Her eyelids fell as she tried to conceal the tears, but he lifted her head. She then pulled away.

"This ain't no flow with the way you look."

"Hormones, Greg. I've been thinking about my mother. I miss her more than I usually say I do." It was at that moment she wished she had her mother, her praying mother, to guide her through raising Sunni, to ask her questions about things that she just didn't want to tell anyone else, things she couldn't dare tell Greg.

"Let me wash you down then. Go ahead and get in."

"I said my period…"

"And *I said* let me wash you down. Massage your back a bit. Go ahead and get in." As she stepped into the tub, Greg took the soap into his hands, lathered it with some water, and began to massage her back. He knew she was hiding something away in her heart, however, he wasn't going to force it out. Greg was more a man who loved everything he needed out of Macon. He'd done that since he'd known her because it was one of the first things he noticed about her personality. She couldn't be forced into anything because it would only push her away. On the contrary, love always worked on her, no matter the situation.

He glanced over at her underwear on the floor. It was clean. Then, he softly whispered into her ear as she faced the faucet. The water violently fell into the tub while his words insisted on becoming the most comforting she'd heard all day. "It's alright. Everything is alright."

Tears streamed down her face as the secret she held close to her heart began to tear itself away from its hiding place. Fear pushed against the massage roaming across her shoulders and spine, and as her neck quivered, he leaned over and kissed her nerves at ease.

"What happened, Macon?"

"I don't know. I don't know what's happening," she whispered. "I do my best, the best I ever knew how to do, you know, and it just doesn't work out." The guilt of losing her first child was creeping into her spirit to join the awesome agony she began to feel that she hadn't raised Sunni right as a mother.

"That happens sometimes."

She reached over to shut the water off and twisted around to face her husband with dreary eyes, but she said nothing.

"Did anything happen? Is Braille doing alright?" he asked as he discontinued rubbing her back and moved from the edge of the tub to his knees to look her square in the eyes. Anger began to boil over inside of him at the thought of someone or something hurting his wife, but once she sensed the rage birthing inside of him, she quickly calmed it.

"Nothing happened, and she's fine. It's just that I don't believe I can handle work and home. It's not like before when I wasn't a mom. I'm tired. I feel overwhelmed."

"Stop, Macon." Removing his hands, he backed away, getting frustrated in an instant from her second guessing her decision after he spent his life savings to start her off on her dreams. "You just started. I'll help out more here at the house until you get into the swing of things, and we will figure it out. This is what you begged for and we need the money back. All I ever worked for," he continued, meaning Sunni, "I have to replace for her future, her education, her…"

"I know…but Sunni has been a handful the last couple of days."

He stood up over the tub, attempting to keep calm about what he just heard, but it became obvious to Macon as he rubbed the top of his head, that he wasn't at all fine with what she said. The fact was that she knew he didn't believe her. She knew that he wouldn't, even if she told him the complete truth. He would fall into denial, just like she had already done, but his would be much worse. He wouldn't be able to handle what Sunni had done or the fact that there was possibly something wrong with her.

"Is this really about Sunni?" he asked suspiciously, staring down at her clean underwear. "You told me your period was on, but what's that? Am I missing something?" He waited for an answer, but Macon was stunned, stomped by her own fabrication and the way it was causing everything she said to be perceived as questionable. "Sunni is a child, and she might misbehave, but what's unusual is how you're just now telling me about it," he stressed, "And you're in here crying, but I'm trying right now,

Macon. I'm nearly broke now after buying that car for you, but I'm trying to put on a good face and keep you happy, baby, but..."

"I know, Greg."

He then kneeled back down. "Whatever you have to say, say it. Don't lie to me. What is it? I want to sleep good tonight, and I wanna sleep with my wife," he stated, kissing her hand and then her arm as the water dripped from her skin. "I'm doing all I can for us, but I need you to be honest with me. You're upset and crying and also hiding something from me that ain't really about Sunni or your period."

"Yes, it is. Sunni's been changing."

"What do you mean changing? She's the same every single time I see her. The same Sunni."

"She's not the same. I mean," she stuttered, "she appears the same, but she's not the same baby we had."

"Children change, don't they? We did. You don't see us walking around in diapers and stumbling across the floor."

"No, we don't change like I'm talking about…not like this," she interrupted, stepping from the tub as he remained kneeled down beside it confused. She grabbed her towel. Finally, he stood, and as she proceeded to wrap it around her body, he noticed even more worry in her eyes. Only with a touch on her shoulders, he was able to gather all of her attention, and she knew she had to say something because he was waiting. She just didn't know what to tell him, nor did she know how to say it without causing the deterioration of her family. It was a fear she'd always hidden as she was traumatized by his unpredictable behavior in the past, and she insisted on not losing him again.

"She kicked me."

"Kicked you?"

She turned to face the mirror, unable to escape his stare as it remained in the reflection. Therefore, she looked into the sink wondering where her next response would lead. "In my stomach."

"In your stomach?"

"Yes. It was the day I told you that she fell against the wall and caused that hole again."

"Sunni did that on accident you told me."

"No, no she didn't," Macon whispered. "She did it purposely, Greg. It was right there after kicking that wall when she got angry with me and kicked me directly in my stomach," she stated softly as she lifted her eyes to look into Greg's through the mirror. "She wanted to cause me pain…and destroy what you fixed. She wasn't even afraid."

"And you're just now telling me this?" he asked, but Macon remained silent. She didn't want to be questioned. She didn't want to fight. All she wanted to do was make everything go away.

"Answer me, Macon. Don't just stare at the walls and in the sink as if I'm not here. I'm right here. I'm that girl's father, and you should have told me this. Did you punish her at all?" he asked, placing all the effort he had into remaining calm and quiet enough as to not awaken Sunni. In reality, he was furious and felt betrayed.

"I didn't punish her. I was going to, but…"

"But?" he asked, turning to face the bathroom window and then back at Macon in total disbelief. "But what? Her butt is what you should have spanked, that's the butt!"

"But she said she didn't remember doing it."

He smiled. "Are you serious, Macon?" Then, he began to laugh, not because anything was funny, but because he didn't know what else to do. He walked out of the bathroom and then turned right back around to enter again. "She took *her* foot, kicked you in the stomach, destroyed the side of the wall on purpose, and then you tell me that she didn't remember doing it?" He turned to walk back out of the bathroom once again just to turn back around to face a situation he didn't believe at all. "And you really want me to believe that?"

"Right after, she didn't remember doing it. It was like she was a different person…like she truly didn't remember."

"Macon," he started, totally not convinced of anything she said based on the first lie she told at the start of the discussion about her period. "I'm going to bed. This doesn't even sound right. What you sound like, and I love you to death, but you sound cra…" he stopped himself. "*It* sounds crazy. *You* sound like you need some sleep."

"Maybe it is," she whispered under her breath. "Maybe I am or maybe she is."

"What?" he asked, unable to catch her words.

"I said I'm sorry for lying to you. I just…"

"Didn't feel like being with me tonight." He turned to walk from the bathroom but stopped with his hand on the door knob, still facing away from her. "Don't go making up elaborate stories like your period is on or Sunni kicked you or any other thing for running out of this house tonight…because you're interested in another man."

Startled by an accusation she felt came out of nowhere, the overwhelming sadness that had gripped her for minutes, suddenly dissipated to be replaced by desperation. "Greg!" When he continued walking, she stepped out and grabbed his arm to which he stopped moving. "Greg, no…no…" But before she even started her statement, he calmly removed her hand to leave her standing there wet and wrapped in a towel. Then, she listened as he entered Sunni's room to wake her.

Quickly, she put on her pajamas and ran to Sunni's doorway. She was already sitting up in his arms, halfway asleep but alert.

"Sunni. Sunni, baby girl?"

"Hmm?"

"I have to ask you a question. You listening?"

She nodded and laid her head on his left shoulder, her eyes still shut and her sleepy face turned toward the doorway where mother stood silently. Greg seemed unaware that she was there watching.

"Listen here. Why did you kick your mother in the stomach and destroy that wall I spent time fixing?"

As soon as Greg ended his question, Sunni's eyes peeled open, and once she saw her mother standing there in the doorway, she was no longer the sleepy little girl she was seconds ago. Her face hardened like rain in freezing weather, and her gaze was as if she saw a stranger at the door instead of her flesh and blood mother. Macon stood there perplexed by the expression on Sunni's face until Sunni turned her head toward her dad's ear and whispered something to him. When she was done, she turned back to face Macon who stood anxious to hear what was said, but Greg didn't say anything back to her. Instead, Sunni only placed her finger to her lips and mouthed *shh* back at her mother with a grin spread across her little face before hugging her father's neck.

Macon moved from the door, placing her back against the wall as she heard Greg tuck her back underneath the sheets. A million things raced through her head from what Sunni told him to how she could convince Greg that something was really wrong. She had only one choice. She had to tell him everything. He finally made it to the doorway.

"Greg, please," she begged.

"She admitted it, and she said that she told you that she was sorry. It was an accident, Macon!" he shouted, fed up with all the secrets for the night. He stormed away with Macon trailing him closely.

"An accident? Whatever she said to you, she's lying" Macon whispered, trying her best to keep her tone low so that Sunni wouldn't hear what she had to say. "I saw her. She's lying and…I'm not lying on my own daughter," she stressed. "She just lied on *me*, not the other way around. I'm telling you, Greg, look at me!" she finally shouted.

"The same way you left out of this house acting one way and came back another? The same way you lied about your flow, and it's not even on?" He waited for an answer but none came. Therefore, he continued. "I suppose the relationship you had didn't end so good tonight, did it? Taking the attention off yourself and putting it on Sunni?"

"That's not the same Sunni we know. Open your eyes, Greg, and there's more…"

"Yeah, my eyes are open, and I don't wanna hear anymore!" His voice elevated to a pitch she hadn't heard in years, and she knew why. The pressure about Sunni was becoming too much, so Macon let the situation die, but he still had one more thing to say. "I see my same Sunni, but who I don't see is my same wife." At that, he exited the house, leaving her standing

there crying in the hallway as Sunni smiled
herself to sleep.

CHAPTER 5

Each night for one full week, Greg walked
inside the house without much of a word besides
speaking to Sunni. There were no kisses good-
bye nor were there any hugs. The only thing that
relayed to Macon that he was still in love with
her were his saddened eyes. Macon understood
that it wasn't an anger that kept him from
speaking, but instead, heartbreak. He'd lost
weight because he didn't have an appetite, and
Macon didn't know what to do. What he was
believing was a lie.

"Greg, talk to me."

"Sure, Macon." He sat on the bed, reading
his Bible. She knew he was finding the strength
to continue on through his doubts about their
relationship and the accusations against his
innocent, little girl.

"I know I lied about my period, but I'm not making excuses to run out on you. You have to believe me. I've been here every night. I haven't gone anywhere, and I don't know why Sunni told you that. It was a lie, falling in line with how I told you that she'd been acting different. You can even talk to Braille…"

"Braille?" he laughed as he turned to face her before turning back into the scripture. "You and Braille. Do you think I don't know about you and Braille and the secrets you all keep? Braille is the last person I will ask about you or anyone you know."

"Greg…"

"Macon, I'm tired. I don't know what you did or doing or whatever. I've been working hard, and I'm tired. As far as Sunni, she said sorry, and since it's been so long, weeks ago, what am I supposed to do even if she did something like that?"

"Just listen to me and stop cutting down everything I try and tell you. I love you, but you aren't giving me a chance."

He shut his Bible and stood from the bed at her words. This was the very first time he'd seen her broken down in tears since the day their communication ceased, and it was the crying that his ears couldn't bear. Walking over, he placed his arms around her, smelled her hair along with her skin as she turned to wipe her tears onto his face to steal a kiss from his lips, the lips she'd missed for days. Grazing was all she received from him as he then backed away and walked down the hallway and into the living room, leaving her with the words, "I still love you." It was there that he slept until the middle of the night when something awakened him.

"Macon?" he called as he shoved himself up from the couch in a daze. It was well after midnight, and he stood up to listen once again, only to hear the noises faintly the second time. "Sunni?" He smiled, recognizing that it was her talking in her sleep for the very first time, but as he prepared to lie back down, another voice sounded out from Sunni's room.

Jumping up from the couch again, he thought he was hearing things, but as he listened closer, he heard his daughter once again. However in the next instant, within seconds, there was someone who sounded like her but slightly different. There was a conversation going on inside Sunni's room, but it didn't sound

like the other person talking was Macon.
Therefore, he walked down the hallway slowly as
the conversation continued, but he hit a crack in
the floor, right outside of Sunni's doorway,
causing the conversation to stop. Quickly, he
turned into the room and flicked on the light.
There was Sunni lying underneath the covers.
He walked over to her bedside, and her eyes were
closed. From there, he looked at her chest and
listened for the sound of her breathing which
sounded calm and relaxed when she was in a
deep sleep. He waited, until finally, her chest
moved. Confused, he looked underneath her bed
and inside her closet and found nothing odd.
Therefore, he made his way back to the room
light, turned to check on Sunni once again before
switching the room light off, causing Sunni's
eyes to open up to the darkness as he left the
doorway. She, then, sat up on the bed listening to
her father walk back into the living room. She
remained upright and still inside the bed for the
rest of the night. The next morning came in
quietly, and not even the brightest light of all the
lights in the sky could disturb her as it rose to its
position.

"Sunni, I'm glad you're up already." her mother whispered, wiping the crust from her eyes and gathering her school clothes from the hanger on the door. When Sunni didn't respond, she called again, this time, tapping her on her foot which was beneath the cover. "Sunni, stop staring and get up, baby. School time." As she reached down to the drawer to get some of Sunni's socks, she noticed no movement at all from her, and she immediately turned around. "Sunni?" she called, reaching over to shake her. Sunni didn't move causing Macon to grow more afraid with each second that passed, shaking Sunni more vigorously at the shoulders as she turned her attention toward the room door when she heard Greg coming down the hallway.

Quickly, she sat on the bed terrified as she continued shaking her daughter who continued to stare off at the closet without blinking or showing any other signs of awareness. "Baby, baby, please. Are you sleeping? Wake up now. You're sitting up…" She pressed on Sunni's back, and it was as stiff as a board. "Oh dear, Father! Baby?" she continued, and just as she was about to call for her husband, he'd already turned into the bedroom.

"Time for school there, sleeptalker," he laughed, but his smile faded away fast as the panic from Macon's eyes struck him into the pits of his soul.

"Greg," she cried, still attempting to gain some sign from her daughter that would show that everything was alright with her. "Greg, Sunni won't move. Something's wrong with her. She won't move! Sunni!"

"Move outta the way, Macon." Faster than he could think, he leaped across the small room and nearly shoved Macon out of the way in order to get to Sunni. "Sunni? Sunni, baby?" He tried to shake her, but she remained still, as if she didn't hear nor see anything else except the closet in front of her.

As Greg removed the sheet from her body, Macon backed further away, feeling something sinister was also there in the room with them. She traced Sunni's line of vision and fearlessly began to follow it, step by step, to where it ended – at the closet. Rapid thoughts of her conversation with Braille sped through her mind, and as she remembered what Braille told her about a man who told her daughter about murder, she stepped directly into the spot where Sunni stared.

Sunni didn't budge. Tears began to flow down Macon's cheeks as she watched her husband give it all he had to set Sunni free from an invisible grip that strangled her movement and mind. It was then that Macon opened her mouth and whispered into the air, "Don't listen." There was so much noise in the room from Greg shouting and wailing for Sunni to come back until she finally shouted through her fears, "Sunni, don't listen!" Greg quickly glanced at his wife who stood there shouting words he didn't quite understand had anything to do with the dire situation they found themselves in, but despite the confusion she saw on his face, she shouted again, remembering her mother's teaching directly from the Holy Bible. "Sunni, you listen to me! Don't listen to him. The voices of strangers you don't follow. Do you hear me! Stop listening!"

Greg, suddenly, dropped his hand from Sunni's back as he felt the firmness of her back slightly slump. After several minutes of them coaxing her to come to, it was only then did Sunni's eyes blink. Then, she lifted her hand to her eyes, wiped them like a waking child, and then spoke.

"Why are y'all crying?"

Greg looked into Macon's eyes, distressed and confused, but she swiftly confirmed what he saw. "I told you. This isn't our same Sunni. I tried to tell you before that I still have things to tell you."

CHAPTER 6

"And I don't care! I said I don't care," he shouted, throwing his fist into the wall. "That's my child, too! Do you hear me?" he furiously charged at her as if he would lose control of himself and hit her like he did the wall. Thankfully, never in life had he done so. The veins in his neck protruded like worms on the thin surface of fine dirt as Macon stood there and took her verbal blows, blows that she knew could get worse over time. She hadn't seen that man in years, but he was back, and she had to learn how to help him back to a better place.

"At first, I didn't think it was going to continue, but then that night I left Braille's, I didn't know what to think or do…"

"Didn't know what to do? Didn't know what to think?"

"No! No!" she shouted, defending herself. "No, I didn't! Are you happy now? I made a mistake, a mistake about everything. Not telling you is on me. Yes, it's on me, but …"

"Yes, it is on you this time. You knew! You knew!"

"This time?" Macon approached Greg despite his rage against her, knowing full well that he was relating this to their stillborn baby years ago. "Sunni isn't dead nor is she dying, Greg. The *last time* was no one's fault, so don't you dare do this again. We won't lose her like we did our other..."

"She's halfway gone already if what you say is true!"

"We can take her to get some help. I've already thought about it."

"With what money? With what, Macon? You ain't earn nothing at that store yet, and I spent all the money I had on that new car for you. That money was for Sunni!"

"How was I supposed to know anything would happen?"

"We never know! We didn't know the last time, and we didn't know this time. All I ever know is it comes, and it sucks all the life we have out of us each time." He then looked at his own wife with disdain. "I should have never listened to you in the first place. All your high hopes for a better future off of nothing. We have to always have to plan for bad times. Always!"

"Well I'm not planning them with you! All that Bible reading you do, walking around like you're a good man, a *God fearing* man, well then show it! Back it up! Where is your faith, huh? You're just like the rest of them who believe in all those witches' tales! You need to back up your belief in God instead of lashing out on me *this time* about something we couldn't do anything about. She's dead. She was dead coming out of me," she yelled, bursting into tears. "There was nothing we could do. I walked into that bathroom and saw nothing but blood and pushed. We didn't kill her, Greg. We loved her, but there was nothing we could do."

Greg's strong, threatening demeanor fell soft as he glanced down at himself, the man he swore he never wanted to become again. He then reached out and embraced his hurting wife, finally understanding full well her own strain while disregarding everything he originally thought she'd been lying about the night he began sleeping on the couch.

"I'm sorry, Macon. Baby, I apologize from the bottom of my heart for everything. I just don't…I didn't know…I didn't understand what you were trying to say, and I couldn't hear you because I didn't want to hear you." Tears fell down his face like he was losing another child to something he couldn't prevent. "I love Sunni."

"I love her, too, but we need you. And it's not you who should be sorry. It's me. But let's stop this, alright? It's not helping anything." She reached up and wiped his tears from his face, and he reciprocated the gesture through his agonizing soft moans for his daughter.

"I can't lose another baby girl. I'm her daddy, Macon. She looked like she was dead, like she was gonna stop breathing, like something had her…the same way it had…"

"Something did, but not death." she interjected. "It's something I wish I'd told you about sooner. That talking that you said she was doing in the middle of the night, it wasn't talking in her sleep. I don't believe that since I've been thinking about everything in totality."

"What else is there…in totality? Nobody was there, Macon."

"She said someone was in the woods...said he said he was gonna kill Braille just like she killed Pumpkin."

The color left Greg's dark brown face, and it was as if he'd seen a ghost. He stared at Macon with loss all in his eyes and replayed the voice he heard inside her room overnight. "No, Macon, no...there was nobody there. I walked in there and she was asleep, Macon."

"I know. But listen to me, please. What if that's what's been going on all along. What if it's in her head, baby? What if that man can't be seen by us," she paused, afraid to insinuate the worst but having no other choice, "Only her?"

Greg backed away from her slowly. "What you sayin'? The only strange voices there are come from..."

Macon stood strong against the sting of those words and confirmed her thoughts aloud. "She only woke up out of that stupor when I told her to stop listening to him. So we got to go get Sunni right now. We're leaving. Ain't no work for you nor me."

"Where are we going?

"We agree that the Lord says the voices of strangers shouldn't be followed, don't we?"

Greg shook his head in agreement, and she continued.

"Now who do we both know about this more than anyone?"

Greg knew exactly who Macon was talking about and he jumped into agreement with her on the decision."That's where we'll take her. We're taking our baby back to the only one who knows more about this than anyone else I've ever met. Even my own Mama used to talk about her, and Lord's willing she's still alive."

Immediately, Macon ran to the telephone and called her job. Breathing like she'd run a marathon, she fought to catch her breath as she watched Sunni from the window sitting outside waiting to go to school. She looked like a normal child, but there was something very wrong, and they were going to catch it before it got out of hand.

"Hello? Hi, this is Mrs. McKinsey. My daughter...she's very sick, and we need to keep her at home today from school which means I can't come in. Will you pass along this message for me since the boss man probably isn't in yet? Is James there?" she continued speaking, one question after another until the person on the other end told her to calm down and hold on. From there, James came to the line. "Hello, James. Thank goodness you are there. I need you to please pass along this message to the boss letting him know that I can't come in today. I will make it up. My daughter is very ill. Very ill, and I have to take her to Maze tonight."

"Maze? There are clinics closer…"

"I know, but I can't take her there. I have to take her to someone who knows this. Will you tell the boss for me?"

"Sure thing. Get there safely. I will pick up your slack, so you don't have to worry."

"Thank you so much. I will pay you back." Macon hung up the phone and rushed to prepare some clothing, calling Sunni back inside the home. "Sunni, come on back inside. We have to leave shortly! Sunni!" she called, but as she waited at the door, Sunni never showed up. "Sunni?" she called again, confused because she'd just seen her when she was looking out of the window. From there, Macon began to panic as she ran back into the house screaming her daughter's name which instantly alerted Greg.

"Where's Sunni?"

"I don't know. She was just outside. We need to find her. She must have wandered off again," she responded, rushing to put on her shoes while Greg already headed out the door with bare feet and chest with only pants on.

From the inside of the home, Macon heard him searching. She followed his voice from the front of the house to the back of it, but when he didn't stop calling, she bolted out of the home and toward the bus stop.

"Sunni! Sunni, the bus is already gone, baby, so come on back. We're going somewhere else this morning," she shouted, convincing herself that Sunni was somewhere around listening. As she turned the corner, she stopped in her tracks. There was no Sunni. Searching the sidewalk and then the street, there wasn't a trace of any children or parents, and as she spun around like a lost soul, there was also no sign of her daughter anywhere, between any houses, bushes nor weeds. She was gone.

Macon grabbed her heart and stumbled back to the house, hoping and praying that Sunni had been found. Passersby looked on and even slowed up their cars, leaning out of the window asking her if she was alright, but Macon just kept jogging as fast as her strength could carry her. Many thoughts ran through her head, like the thoughts of someone snatching Sunni from the yard or either Sunni being led away by those same voices that kept her captive. Maybe she was somewhere wanting to be rescued but trapped inside herself again or either trapped by a real life man, the same man she said was there with her in the woods. Maybe he *was* real.

"Greg! Is she in the house? Greg!" she shouted as she burst through the door. There was no sign of Greg or any sign of Sunni. "Oh God..." she called as she spun around in one spot, searching for a clue, any clue, to where Sunni may have been. That was when Greg ran back through the front door, causing her to halt spinning around empty handed, hoping that her child had returned to her arms. When she saw Greg dash for his car keys, she knew her arms would remain empty.

"Get your keys. You go one way, and I'll drive the other way. She's around here somewhere."

Macon stood there with her arms outstretched, feeling the emptiness that she'd only felt once before in her life, but this time, it was much worse. "We shouldn't have let her go outside," she mumbled. "I should have kept her…"

"Macon!" She snapped out of her daze as Greg handed her the car keys and continued at an amplified pitch. "Macon, I need you to wake up and go…drive to the school to see if she's there. I will drive around and ask everyone I see if they've seen her. Everybody around here knows us, so…"

"Yeah, okay. Everything is going to be fine," she responded, not because she truly felt like things would come together and be okay but because she was so accustomed to saying it. Only this time, she was even afraid of the robotic words that exited her mouth. Instead of convincing Greg, she was also convincing herself.

She took the keys and in her pajamas, left the home. From her rearview mirror, she watched as Greg pulled out from the front of what was once their cozy home, and she immediately drowned in a rush of tears, making it nearly impossible for her to see clear enough to drive. "Sunni," she cried. "Please, come back. I didn't know. Mama didn't know. Just please come back." The guilt of knowing that Sunni had already drifted away from Braille's home made her feel like she should have known never to leave her outside for a couple of minutes. Although, she'd never drifted off from home before, her knowledge of the way Sunni had been on a steady decline wouldn't let her dismiss how foolish the decision was.

The school yard was further down the road, and although she saw a few buses, she didn't see if Sunni's bus had already come or gone. Whatever the case was, the bus wasn't going to give her the solid answer she needed about her child's whereabouts, so she parked her car and ran into the school in hopes to find Sunni, totally ignoring those who were on the sidewalk and the schoolyard gawking at her as her pajamas shook with the wind. It was obvious that there was trouble brewing to most of the onlookers, and one of them immediately ran after her.

"Ma'am. Ma'am, is everything alright? Do you need some help?"

"I need to find my daughter. She wasn't supposed to go to school today, and when I looked outside, she was gone. She's only in kindergarten, and I think she may have gotten on the bus, but I'm not sure. Just want to get her and make sure she's alright."

"Okay…well, I'm a teacher here at the school. Come with me." She took her by the hand and rushed her through the school. When they reached the classroom, one quick scan of the children revealed the worst. Sunni hadn't gotten off the bus with the other students.

"Sunni!" Greg shouted from his car window. He drove slowly down each street, and when he got to the middle of the street, jumped out and knocked on the doors. If someone was at home, he asked to search through their yards. Every person was kind enough, allowing him to walk through and some even invited him inside to look around in order to set his mind at ease.

When he found no trace of Sunni, he went back to the house to wait on Macon, feeling like more than likely that was where Sunni was, at school. However, as he impatiently waited, there was something in his soul urging him to keep looking, but not where he originally thought. Immediately, he stepped back outside and turned to the right. There was a major road about six houses down and then nothing but pure field of high grass. If someone Sunni's size was walking, they couldn't be seen, and if they kept walking on through, they hit the next houses in the other neighborhood. It was where Braille lived.

He ran back into the house and looked at the list of numbers that Macon kept near the telephone. From there, he called but ended up dialing so fast that he selected the wrong numbers. After hanging up and waiting on the tone once more, he dialed again. As he watched the dial fall back into place on the rotary phone, it felt like each number took forever to be received, but once he was done, he listened. The phone was ringing…but it kept ringing. There was never an answer. He moved the phone from his ear and slammed it against the wall before running back out of the house.

Instead of taking his car, he charged toward the huge open field that was layered with some of the highest and most beautiful grass that could be seen for miles. Today, the grass didn't seem so friendly as Greg approached. Instead it looked to him like the wickedness of switches as the grass danced without music, demented. The grass was beautiful in appearance but enticing like the devil, just right for a child to take a step inside and run and play, not thinking of the dangers that could lurk beneath the beauty of it all.

As he ran through the grass that reached slightly beyond his thigh, he continued to call out for his daughter. His heart filled with strength as he refused to stop calling through the grass until he completed his race toward the other side of the field. He listened to his own voice return to him empty as his feet stomped upon the laughter and taunting coming from the ground. He attempted to shake the thought, but it kept coming back to him – how the grave called for his first daughter and how it's possibly laughing again, its mouth wide open for the second. If he could kill death, he would, but as he ran and searched, he loudly quoted the scriptures in order to halt the haunting thoughts of a repeated loss, reminding himself that Jesus already defeated that enemy called death a long time ago. With tears running down his face, he stopped at the edge of the field and looked back into the ground, shouting, "No matter what, we live! Today, you won't take Sunni, and you won't take her tomorrow or ever!"

The vessels powered through his chest and neck like a deranged monster, and an anger fueled his fight to destroy whatever it was that was constantly coming after his family like a never ending disease that lay dormant and reared its ugly head only when it felt like manifesting its destruction. His heart raced faster than it ever has before, and he fell to his knees, his body burdened by a situation that was strong-arming every bit of control he ever had surrounding his family. He planned and prepared day in and day out for battles, but he never thought that the ultimate war would end up being another one after his own child. The chaos pulled on every ounce of faith that he had inside of him, but he gained the strength once more to shove back against the doubt and fear, lifting himself from the ground, only to race forward once again toward the destination that could have been another false finish.

Approaching the house, he slowed to notice that the door was already ajar, but it made no sense to him because he'd already called the home and no one picked up. He remembered what Macon told him during their conversation back at the house, that Braille felt someone was going to kill her and that those words came from Sunni herself. Therefore, before he walked any closer, he searched for anything he could use to attack someone. He found nothing in the yard except a large stone that he picked up and gripped as tightly as he could. From there, he stepped up into the doorway, letting himself inside.

Tempted to call her name, he instead held his peace, assuming that was the best option although he knew Braille well enough to know that he could possibly get knocked down if she was startled because she wasn't one to back down from anyone, not even a man. He also knew that although she was prone to leaving her door unlocked, with what he heard about how terrified she was, he doubted it would be open like it was. Threat or no threat, it was never ajar, maybe unlocked but never swinging open. The screen door was even flat against the house. It wasn't like her.

At the short hallway, he paused and heard the sound of hard breathing, like someone was asleep, but it wasn't a full snore. Thankful and dropping his guard slightly, he took a deep breath and continued to walk a bit faster down the hallway and into the room to awaken his wife's cousin who'd obviously mistakenly left the door open. However, when he knocked and pushed the room door prepared to awaken her, it was the person he was in search of that he found.

Greg stood there in silence as the door flew open and the doorknob banged against the wall, creating a sound like a firecracker that radiated through the four walls. A snoring Braille awakened, startled to see Greg standing and staring from her bedroom door. He didn't say a word, but stood there in some sort of shock at something next to her, on the other side of the bed. Quickly, as she noticed the horror in his eyes, she flipped her body over to see what he was looking at. Her eyes landed on a very familiar face. It was the face of Sunni.

She stood towering over Braille with a knife secured in both of her small hands with her arms lifted above her head. The sunlight sent a fresh gleam across the sharp blade that stole a portion of clear vision from Braille as the knife tore down into the mattress, missing a screaming Braille by only a slice of brown hairs that was trapped by the knife inside her pillow. Greg leaped across the bed, nearly tackling young Sunni, ripping the knife from her small hands and watching it fall to the ground. Braille stumbled completely off the other side of the bed, grabbing a lamp that was on the nightstand as she scrambled back to her feet.

"She tried to kill me! She tried to kill me! I told you…I told you from the very beginning," she screamed out of breath, glaring viciously at the young girl she once loved just the other day. "Get her out of here before I kill her myself!"

"Braille!"

"Get her out!"

"Your door was open, Braille…" he stuttered hoping to dismantle the fury building in Braille's heart before staring back at Sunni who stood there expressionless, like she was lost in a trance, so he addressed her. "How did you get in here? Why were you standing up in here with a knife to cousin Braille?" His words were pointed directly at her, but those same words seemed to avoid Sunni altogether as she behaved as she heard nothing her father asked. "Sunni? Answer me," he ordered, but she only started crying before saying something that nearly knocked the wind from him.

"What did I do wrong? I was doing everything right, and he said he was proud of me."

"He was proud of you?" he whispered, but Braille interrupted thunderously.

"It's him. It's that *man*," she strained. "It's that same man that told her he was gonna kill me back in them woods, and he must have let her in my house. He told her to do it. He told you to do it, didn't he? Answer me, Sunni!" she ordered, banging the lamp against the wall until it broke in two, revealing extremely sharp edges. She held it inside her hand like a weapon. "You tell me or both of you dead. Both of y'all in my room, how I know both of you ain't trying to take my life, but I'll come at you both this day right here I will!"

"Now you wait a minute. You won't be touching my daughter. Now…I know what she was doing in here is the worst thing, but this ain't Sunni and you know it."

"You better be lucky you got her in your arms because I may not have brought her in this world, but she will be leaving out before I just sit back and let her kill me like she butchered Pumpkin. I done told Macon that she cursed, and she didn't want to hear it. And guess what else? She gonna kill you, too."

There was complete silence. Even the Sunni's whimpers ceased. Greg made the decision to move past a visibly shaken and defensive Braille, and even though he wanted to calm her down, he understood that she had every right to feel how she felt, family or no family. As he passed by Braille, he saw her look at something on the floor near the bedroom door, but before he realized exactly what she was looking at, Sunni spoke.

"No. Just you. I was just gonna kill you. Not my mama and not my daddy, just you, *cousin* Braille. Just you."

"Get that child outta my house! Don't you ever come back in here, or I will kill you at first sight. You mark every one of my words – I will kill you so quick the memory of your own short life will be gone from the face of this earth."

Greg's fist tightened at her words, and he spun around to face Braille for the last time, nearing attacking her himself. "This is your cousin, my daughter! This is your own flesh and blood, and you…"

"And *she*!" she interrupted furiously. "And *she* got my own knife to my throat! You go rationalize that since you and Macon so good at it. I see one thing and one thing only – she tried to kill me dead." Then, she took a few more steps before reaching down to pick up what was on the floor. It was Macon's spare key…for Braille's house. "And you see this?" she asked, lifting the key in the air. "You tell me that she ain't pull the wool over your eyes yet? That ain't no little girl you're dealing with right there. That…that's something else. It's something else in there, now get out." She shoved the key in her pocket as he backed away from her and out of the front door, relieved to have found his daughter, but taking a tremendous loss to the heart from the state of his family, the entire family.

"Oh thank God, Greg," she stated as she ran down the hallway to a happy-go-lucky Sunni, grabbing her to give her the tightest hug she'd ever given her. "Oh, Sunni, don't you ever go off like that. Where were you? Greg?" she beckoned him, awaiting an answer that would calm her anxiety-ridden curiosity.

"She was out there somewhere," he stated, choked up, but ready to leave. Macon noticed his disturbed demeanor and rushed to him, this time, with Sunni in her grasp, afraid to let her go. "Greg, what happened? Where was she?"

"We're leaving right now. We're headed back to Maze like we planned."

"To Maze before you tell me what happened?" She yanked him by the arm, and he froze only to stare directly in front of him at the wall. "Now tell me what happened? Where did you find her?" She knew something was wrong, seriously wrong, and she also understood that it could be something that he didn't want to repeat – the same way she didn't want to repeat anything about Sunni to anyone but God. She glanced at Sunni who stared back at her silent father, but when he spoke, her eyes fell to the floor.

"She was a Braille's."

"Braille's? She walked over there?"

"Yeah, she did."

"Well, thank God she went there, or she could have gotten herself hurt or worse," she sighed. "Don't you ever walk off again, Sunni. I know that's your cousin, but you can't just go off like that. You know better. I'd already been up to the school and …"

"She used your key to open Braille's door. When she went inside, she had a knife to Braille as she slept. Tried to kill her. I saw the whole thing." He continued as he walked from the room. "We're blessed by God that Braille, with the type of woman she is, didn't take her from us."

Macon dropped her daughter's hand in horror, falling to her knees in agony, crying tears that she'd never cried before. With the way Braille felt and the threats she'd received, there was no way she would let not even her own cousin get away with an attempt on her life, no matter how young or old. It was their way. It had always been their way, and Braille wasn't going to change it. Even though she didn't bring any children into the world, she wouldn't hesitate to take them out, especially if they started the battle.

Quickly, she took hold of Sunni and marched her to the telephone, but before she was able to pick it up, Greg was there to move her hand away.

"No, Greg," she stated weeping, "I have to fix this."

"Ain't no way you can fix it."

"What do you mean? She knows something is wrong, just a little bit off with Sunni, so just let me…"

"I said no!" His hands trembled and his voice quaked, like he was going to implode at any second, and that was what it took to make Macon stumble backwards in fear of what would happen next. "Now," he continued softly, pulling himself together. "I just told you there is no way that you or I can fix how Braille feels right now. We can only fix how we feel and what we do with ourselves and Sunni. Leave Braille there. I know y'all are like sisters, but you got to leave her for a long while until this rage wears off. There's nothing you can say," he continued, severely disturbed by everything that had transpired, "because Sunni said enough."

She hesitated, "What did she say?"

"She said that she was aiming to kill only her, not anybody else, just her." He looked down at Sunni. "Come on to the car." He left Macon standing there in tears, looking at the phone on the wall.

CHAPTER 7

They drove. The only thing that was heard was the sound of Sunni's light snoring once again. She was always one to fall asleep during a long drive, and this one was about an hour to the city from where Macon was born and Greg was raised during his teenage life. No one in Maze had any idea that they were coming. They were just going to show up, hopefully get the help they felt they needed, and return to work in the next twenty-four hours.

"It's still early," Macon finally stated about thirty minutes into the drive down the long road. "By the time we get there, everyone will be busy at work."

"That's the plan. I don't want anyone to know our business down here, or they will look at us...Sunni...differently, like she's not even family. All we need to see is the person that we came to see."

"Well, I don't think Old Lady Lyves will tell a soul about why we are coming to see her. Besides," she paused, "not even she knows we're coming. I just hope she's there."

He looked to his left as the sun began to get higher in the morning sky. At that moment, he felt relieved, like instead of losing his daughter, he was on the road saving her. "She'll be there. Sunni will be just fine." However, as he spoke, Macon noticed that his voice sounded weaker, so she faced him and that was when she noticed his tears. He continued talking.

"You should have seen her there, Macon. You should have seen her. She'd taken your keys, and went in that house, stood over Braille and was about to kill her with that knife. It was like someone else was holding her arms up there, but she was holding on to that knife like she didn't even care. If I hadn't gotten there when I did..."

"But you did. You got there right on time, Greg. Just keep driving. I thank God you saved her... and Braille's life. We...all three of us...are going to be fine. We will. Let's just go where God leads us."

The rest of the journey was filled with his silent tears, and only when they pulled up to the quiet cul-de-sac at the end of the winding dirt road did he wipe his face as a façade that he was fine. Soon, they were knocking on a bright green door that could have use a fresh coat of paint, and Old Lady Lyves answered. No matter how much they tried to conceal how upset they were, she sensed immediately that something was wrong, beyond their fake expressions of peace. She opened the door with a huge smile on her face because she remembered them as they grew up. Even their names, she remembered. She was the type to know everyone by name because she was raised to remember, believing that you couldn't count on paper to do it for you, especially how her parents grew up. Everything was at the tongue and on the tongue and traced by the tongue. Anything else could be destroyed.

"Greg and Macon," she laughed, hitting herself on the thigh with her palm of her hand. Her large veins protruded from underneath what was now very thin and aged skin, but even though she was in her nineties, she was still getting around slowly but good. Her face barely had a wrinkle on it while her hair, although very thin, was silky, curly white, like the heavens had delivered her a mighty crown early on. As she held the door open, Greg reached in and propped the heavy door onto his arm, so that she could let go.

"You still remember us, Mama Lyves? We haven't seen you in so long," he said as he beckoned Macon and Sunni inside. "We apologize for coming to see you so early unannounced, but we…"

She lifted her hand up in the air as she mosied back to the high back chair in her living area. The place was medium sized and painted blue, a light blue, on the inside with the strong odor of moth balls and even hot cinnamon apples. There was a large sized rug on the scuffed up hardwood floor and heavy, cream colored curtains that draped the windows. Looking hard enough revealed the lines of dust at the end of the curtain that swept up below the large windows. It was obvious that she hadn't been able to keep up with housekeeping as she used to do when she was younger. There was so much talk around the town twenty or so years back about how she kept an immaculate home, how a person could eat from the floors. Time had worn her down, but it was obvious, apart from the draperies, that she did the best she could with no obvious help in her old age.

"Nobody calls me. That's quite alright, long as they come. People tend to visit when they can, just to visit, but I understand that most young folk like yourself have lives to pay for and children to raise up. Ain't got time to just pay visits to an old lady like myself all the time when you got bills to pay instead," she replied calmly as she plopped down into the cushioned chair, "'Lest they need me for something. Either way, I'm at the point in my life that I'm supposed to be needed, not necessarily wanted, but needed. That don't make me sad though. What makes me sad is when folk act like they don't need me neither. That there is when my heart go acting funny, and they gets into trouble, thinking they know what they don't know nothing 'bout." She then picked up a bowl full of the cinnamon apples that scented the room. "Got a whole pot. Help yourself there." Then, she completely stopped speaking and looked toward Sunni.

"I'm sorry," Macon immediately stated after giving Old Lady Lyves the utmost respect of not cutting her off during conversation. "We live out of town and…"

"No, I know where ya live there, child. But since you sorry, let me tell you what I'ma need from you after this here visit so you can make it up to me." She then put on a big smile, reached over and touched Macon's hand, and pulled her down onto the chair right next to her as Greg took a seat on the couch with Sunni. "Call me every week to let me know how you doing. That will satisfy me just fine. I know you love me, just busy is all. I used to be young, too. Just remember me. Just remember me, let me know how things going and such. These phones here keep people further away from each other, but I suppose that's the way now. People can move and call, and that's what they call keeping in touch. I remember when I never had no phone. Had to see people face to face. Always *knowed* if somebody needed something because you could see 'em. That phone be one that can hide the truth, make stuff sound good when it ain't."

"Yes ma'am. I can only pray we live to see and be your age and know what you know. You are a blessing to us all out of Maze…our only connection to those things we have yet to learn about…" she glanced hastily at Sunni before continuing, "Things we can't see."

"What's that, chile?" she asked, relaxing her back on some pillows that Greg quickly got up and fluffed for her. "Thank you, son."

"Well, Mama…"

"Send that child in the back room. Got no business hearing grown folk talking," she ordered. "They learn too fast, too fast 'fore they brains know what's going on and they end up in trouble behind what we say," she laughed.

"But it's about her."

"Maybe and even though it's about her, it's still something she don't need to take into her ears 'lest it's inspected first. Words…they can do one or two things."

"What's that, Mama Lyves?"

"Bless or curse…depending on how that baby understands a thing. Call 'em bad, they stay bad. Call 'em shy, and they stay shy. Children this here age tend to stay what you make 'em in conversation 'til they learn otherwise, and it takes too long a time for them to get wise enough to learn the other side. That's the reason it be best to let 'em leave the room so they can be themselves and not get hurt up by the beginning of things."

"Go on, Sunni, and stay put back there."

"Got some toys back there, sugarfoot," Old Lady Lyves laughed as Sunni got up and walked back to the room anticipating toys she'd never played with a day in her life. "Made 'em myself." When she heard the child settle down, she turned to face Greg. "You told the child to stay put like she's a running one?"

"She did this morning," he answered, sitting at the edge of the sofa while bouncing his knee up and down like a nervous wreck. "We couldn't find her earlier this morning, and so we decided to come here, right away, to see what's wrong with her."

"Sound like a curious child to me, one that don't like to be confined. Nothing that a switch out there won't cure," she chuckled. "I got my share of them I tell you. Stung me right good back into shape. Ain't take much. One, maybe two, licks to the back thigh," she laughed. "I 'member them days when I was cuttin' up."

Macon then, moved to where Greg sat, scooted up to the edge of the sofa and placed her pocketbook on the floor. "Mama Lyves, there's much more than that. She's been talking to people who aren't there." Although she thought that would create a response from Mama Lyves, it didn't. Instead, Mama Lyves just sat there

171

with her palms together on her thighs seeming to wait on more information to make her move to say something. Macon continued, "She lets a man tell her what to do, and she does it. She thought he was in the same room with us, but he wasn't there at all. There was nothing there. She even killed a pet, and just this morning, she held a knife to her own flesh and blood cousin without remorse. That's what she'd run to do. She ran to commit a murder that somebody told her to do. She pretends she doesn't remember things, but she does." Macon's hands scrub together like aluminum on a dirty pan, and Mama Lyves noticed the motion which told the story of a worried mother. "I can't explain it, but it's not normal. It can't be."

"Sure it is, child. It's as normal as the two eyes under your forehead," Old Lady Lyves spoke to their shock. They couldn't believe that she'd called Sunni's actions normal, so Macon continued, in order to gain more insight on why she was saying what she said.

"My cousin believes she's cursed, like some kind of witch has cursed her," she spoke, hanging her head low in sadness and shame as the tears began to tell the story of how broken her heart was behind her family being torn down to nothing behind what was going on. "She even said we should abandon her because no good will come on our end if we keep her with us. Mama Lyves, to tell you the truth, I don't believe in witches, much less a cursed child. That stuff is nonsense…especially since I was raised a Christian who believes in the power of the Lord."

"Folks been acting like she been acting since I been living and gonna keep doing it, too," Old Lady Lyves interjected. "As far as them witches…well, the Lord himself knows about witches, too, Macon. That's 'xactly why it says in the Word that rebellion is as the sin of witchcraft. See that there? If witchcraft wasn't so, it wouldn't be in there, now would it? That witchcraft, that be people crafting up stuff, making stuff, even giving they souls up to the devil there. That's witchcraft, child. But I reckon what you telling me about that little girl might not be that. No, I don't believe it be that witchcraft."

"Mama Lyves, she even kicked me, lied to me, and I didn't want to make too much of it until this morning when she was staring at something but couldn't hear us, even though we pushed and pulled on her, she just wouldn't come out of it." As she spoke, Greg nodded, encouraging her to complete the story. "She wouldn't come out of it until I told her not to follow the voices of strangers. That was when she broke."

There was a box of tissue located on the floor right next to where Old Lady Lyves sat, and she reached down to wipe the water coming from her left eye. She wasn't crying, but her eyes, particularly one, continued to drain water, thus the need for the box of tissue. "It been seeming to me all my life that when the Word of God says not to follow strange voices, it means any voice that ain't His and any way that ain't His. And if it ain't His voice, it's the devils or demons, not just the people they use, but them, too. They talk, too. The Bible wasn't always talking about voices like you and me, Macon. He was probably talking about them other voices that come from the invisible... but I can tell you if a *visible* stranger come down the street there, it be best I don't open my door either," she laughed. "So it kinda works both ways now don't it, including with obedience and disobedience. Mama and daddy say don't do this and that curious voice says to do it anyway. Which do you listen to? The one you know best, the one you've known the longest I reckon. The voice you listen to can lead you right and or it can lead you wrong, I 'spect." The hot cinnamon apples had already cooled down, so she took a spoonful, and they watched as her chubby cheeks bounced around as she chewed. Suddenly, she burst out in a giggle. "See, I gots no teeth except for one. I have to soften all my food for my old gums. If you come back round, bring me some more bananas. The ones round there turning black...can't keep 'em long," she drifted off as Macon anxiously nodded.

"Tell you what. People nowadays done started falling away from what I believe...what the Word say. I'm gonna tell you anyway 'cause it's the truth. Whatever be wrong with her, you got to heal her from the inside out. That's how the devil kill folk, ain't it? Starting from the inside," she stated, waving her hand toward her body and then away from it, "Then he go out. Because of that, see, it only makes sense to get the healing from the inside out, too. That's even how my own teeth rot! It start from the inside 'fore you see that black on the outside," she laughed, nearly dropping her cinnamon apples on the floor. Greg quickly reached over to catch them, and she nodded, patting his hand and smiling. "That devil is at the root of what is going on with that child. It's gonna take Jesus to heal that root and restore that baby because some demon done took root. While y'all was talking all her life, it was talking, too. That demon ain't no stranger to her. He came early to her and probably been talkin' to her more than you and him put together. That's why she can't hardly tell the difference between what it tell her or what you tell her. How old she?"

"Five. Just starting school and everything," Macon blurted out, anxious to hear more although devastated at her worst fears coming from Old Lady Lyves's mouth. "Do you think we should get somebody to look at her? Like in a hospital…one of those new mental ones they've been building for…"

"Don't you dare not!" Her foot slammed against the floor so hard that the wood shook, and she shot a stare at Macon that made her feel smaller than a child herself. "Don't you not ever take her in no place like that, you hear me? Place like that ain't fit for nobody. Not nobody, especially our kind. Don't you forget!" She raised her hand and pointed wildly at both Macon and Greg, nearly coming off of her chair. "They kill us there. Ever since they made 'em for us, they been killing us, making us worse. You hear me? They kill us." With quivering lips, her entire demeanor changed from laughter and listening to heartache and despair. "Keep that girl from the new hell they put on this earth. That there place is the Hades only they know 'bout. They stuck my brother. Took his head with a hole. Nothing was wrong with him, just a heavy tongue and a sleep ear, and they make him crazy. Hittin' him, not feedin' him. They make us black folk sick in them walls. If you think she sick now, you wait. Let her be, and do as I tell you. Them there doctors over there in that mental place don't mean black folk no good. I seen it for myself."

"But what if she gets worse before getting better, Mama Lyves? I mean, I been praying for her, but it seems like…"

"Hush, Macon." She paused before continuing, being certain that she wouldn't be interrupted anymore. "Now, since you keep talking about 'em, I suppose on certain things what them mental doctors down there do is called suppressing a thing, suppress the body so it won't act out what the voices tell it. That there can help hold your baby body down for a spell if done right with a kind doctor, but, you see, they, all them doctors, only go from the outside in. The voices still there," she stressed. "Them doctors only hold the *body* down. They don't cure it, and even sometimes, especially with our kind, they like to 'speriment, do all kind of things to us that destroys us anyway. A mental house ain't nowhere for our kind, not with these white men there. No, we takes care of our own. It's been that way for the longest and that's the way it should stay. I done lived through it, and I know," she stated forcefully. "Don't let them start 'sperimenting with that child when God done told us what it is already. Like I say from the start, them doctors only go from the outside in. To start at the root though, the root, everything will heal, and power like that come from the Almighty God. I know. See here...this thing can't no doctor see into," she stated, pointing at her head. "They got to wait for it. Can't do nothing but wait for it to reveal what's there. Doctors got to see signs. Jesus...He already know. Get my Bible from there. Let me show you."

Greg saw a big, white Bible sitting on the sofa table right next to him, so he obediently reached around and grabbed it as the tears rolled down Macon's face. She knew what scripture she was speaking of, however, she'd been hoping she was wrong ever since she started noticing Sunni's behavior.

"First, son, turn to that John gospel there. John chapter ten and read me that first verse out loud."

Greg cleared his throat and read, "He that enters by the door is the shepherd of the sheep."

"Now keep going."

"Verily I say unto you, he that enters not by the door into the sheepfold, but climbs in some other way, the same is a thief or robber. But he that enters by the door is the shepherd of the sheep. To him the porter opens, and the sheep hear his voice. He calls his own sheep by their name, and leads them out. And when he puts forth his own sheep, he goes before them, and the sheep follow him for the sheep know his voice. And a stranger they will not follow but flee from him for they know not the voice of strangers."

"Stop right there. You see that? It say the difference between the thief and the one who enters in by the door. Read on down to find out that Jesus be the door, so He lets in the right voice. Any other way they come in your house, or your body, be the wrong voice to take something from you, rob you, even kill you. Something got in there to take your baby. It ain't come in right, so you know it's from wrong.

Ain't sent from God at all. Now turn on over to
Legion there in Mark chapter five. Read it for
me, and you listen to it yourself."

As he read and finally finished, she then
summarized what he said. "That man that came
up there to Jesus had spirits named Legion on the
inside of him making him act crazy and all out of
order, nobody could control that man neither.
See that? That there," Old Lady Lyves stated,
pointing to the pages. "How did that Legion, a
demon of many demons, get inside that man,
huh? Can you tell me that? It wasn't by Jesus
because it was cast out by Jesus. It came in there
through a window, like a thief. See that there.
That evil voice, them voices that had that man
cutting his own self, destroying his own body,"
she stressed, "And no man could control his
actions. Now, that there sounds like your child,
but not to that degree. And you see something
else?" She leaned forward and widened her
eyeballs so that the brown pigment spots showed
all over the whites. "Them Legion, them demons
inside that man…they talk! They was driving
him crazy, making him do things he wouldn't do
in the normal liking. Them demons ain't talk to
everybody, just the man that they was inside of,
but Jesus caught them at they root! They was
scared of the King." She slapped her hands

together and started laughing. "Then he cast 'em out. The man fell clean, ain't it? That there means that demons are strangers with they own voices that don't come through our door Jesus, and those same demons, just like they was false prophets walking around us in the full light of day, talk. They have voices, and only Jesus could identify that it was an unclean spirit, spoke back to it…it wasn't the man talking. It was Legion." Then Old Lady Lyves sat back in the chair. "Only Jesus can get to the root of that in your child, and you got to fast and pray for her first. Them kind be stubborn and strong. They even listening to us now," she said, going from a stern seriousness to a lighthearted, gummy smile although the topic wasn't at all to be joked about. "It be like a worm or them things that live inside your body comfortable, but you got to run 'em out somehow, less it kill you. An aspirin will work to keep the fever down, but that don't mean the problem gone. You got to have the right type of medicine to run that worm out. Understand that now? The root. You got to get to the root…even if you got the aspirin or not. Faith goes to the root of any matter."

"You can't do this on your own. Jesus can, and He can do it through you by your own faith. No telling how long you got to fast and pray and then cast out, but do it in the name of Jesus. These demons come back to fight for they turf, just like you fighting for yours, except they caught you in your blindside. She got to resist them, and they flee, but she's a little girl, so you got to do the fighting for her, you hear? In the meantime…"

"Excuse me, Mama Lyves, but why can't we do it now? Why can't we tell it, or them, to go now? Just cast it out like in the Bible," Greg asked.

"Well, look atcha!" she laughed. "You was already shook up at the door when I let you in. Saw right through you, and Macon here. She was just about in tears. You just ain't ready yet, child. Fast…pray…go to the Lord…lose sleep gaining strength and praying. Jesus will fight this battle. He promised, ain't it? Now as I said before, in the meantime, you got to keep her steady as best you can, watch her, feed her good, keep her good company, read her Jesus, raise her with Him because He isn't just a part of the family. He *is* the family because God created it, didn't He, now?" she grinned, but then she pushed herself up from the chair as she wiped the grin from her face as she looked to the floor, obviously remembering something from the past.

"I don't imagine that this will be different from anything else. Had only seen one other person like that in my whole, long life, and you can thank the mighty God that you see it when she little and easier to contain. Grown folks run from you, can hurt you bad, too. Yep, hard to get 'em and keep 'em in one spot. Now, let me get my oil here," she sighed. "Just a minute. Run back there and get her. Go on. She won't bite."

When Old Lady Lyves returned, Sunni was sitting there quietly on her father's lap. She didn't appear afraid of anything, and it was clear to Old Lady Lyves that the little girl had no idea what was about to happen to her.

"Y'all gone on and leave out. Shut the big door behind you."

"Leave out?" Macon questioned, wondering about why she had to leave Sunni alone. "I mean, I trust you, Mama Lyves, but why do I have to do that?"

"It's the best thing. Full faith, unwavering faith, and I ain't worried nor am I scared. You're scared. Though you have faith, you're still looking at your child and not the problem, not the root. That there is why you got to get out. That's how it been tricking you all this time, ain't it? It got you doubting this could actually be happening to your child because it hides inside her. Ain't I right?" she asked, and after they understood what she was speaking of, they turned to walk from the house. As they left, the first words from Old Lady Lyves's mouth was, "Father God in the name of Jesus…"

She walked the blessed oil all around the child, and as she prayed, she suddenly took the child by the head and poured the oil from the top of her hair until it covered the towel that had been draped across the back of her neck. Afterwards, although she was elderly, she got down on her knees and held the child in a huge cradle of prayer, lifting her up to the Lord, but she still hadn't cast out what needed to be cast out. Finally, she stood to her feet and stood directly in front of Sunni who was wiping the oil from her head onto her hands.

"Now loose her. Loose her now, in the name of Jesus, the Son of the Living God. Hide not yourself because we know you are there. Who are you, inside of this child?" When she received no answer, she spoke again. "Loose her in the name of Jesus. Father God, please cast any and all evil that is not of you, out of this young girl this hour because you know who it is, and

only you can remove it. What is your name?"
she then asked as the child looked on,
undisturbed by what was going on. "I asked you
that is inside the child, what is your name? Who
are you called by?" Then, Old Lady Lyves
moved in closer to see into the reflection of the
young girl's eyes. She felt she had been around
the spirit before. "You are familiar, aren't you?
You been here before, haven't you?" she
confirmed, without any solid proof except what
she felt inside her spirit. Immediately, she
backed far away and demanded it leave, "You
are not invited inside my home or this little …"

"Shh," the child responded quietly, over
Old Lady Lyves's words. "Shh," she then
mumbled once again before she started swinging
her dangling legs. "Shh. I can't say who he is."

"Tell him to talk to me, and he can tell me
himself. Ain't it a man talking to you, baby?"

"Shh…he's telling you to shh, old lady,"
Sunni responded in a crisp, sure tone unlike the
coy voice seconds ago. Her feet continued to
dangle from the seat, but her eyes were held
steady onto Old Lady Lyves's eyes.

"I see there that he got you sayin' things
for him, but if he so powerful, tell him to face the

Son of the Living God Jesus Christ. In the name
of Jesus…"

"Mama!" she screamed, struck with fear or
so it seemed, and it took no time for her mother
to come rushing into the house. As Old Lady
Lyves watched them rush inside at their
daughter's calls and cries, she slowly sat back
down on her chair, observing how much power
the situation had over them and how little power
they had over it. It wasn't Sunni. No child had
ever been afraid of the name of Jesus. It was
what was in her that was afraid, causing a
distraction.

"Well, I see there that you two needs more
time," the old lady disappointingly stated. "This
wasn't a test for her, but for you."

"What's wrong, Sunni? Mama Lyves?"
Macon asked out of breath from the anxiety
thrown upon her by the shrieking sounds of
Sunni.

"There ain't a thing wrong except that
thing in her don't wanna be cooped up in here
with my old, God fearing self because I didn't
invite it. It ain't allowed. Got the girl doing and
saying things for him, almost like she think it's
herself I suppose. You watch after her. Pray all

the time and fast. That one done found a home it likes, and it wants to take her down back to the pits with him. It hides itself really good, so keep watch and pray."

"But what happened?" Greg shouted, confused about why Sunni was so worked up and struggling to leave the home, but his shouting ceased when Old Lady Lyves picked up a cane and struck the wall as hard as her arms could.

"Shut your mouth in my house with all that yellin'! You keep quiet, and remember what I said." She leaned forward forcefully and pointed the end of the cane directly at Sunni while her eyes remained locked on Greg. "This action here only *looks* like your baby girl, but you can't treat her like it always. Pay attention. She changes slight enough that even the wind cringes when he talks through her. That thing talkin' to her be in the air. Pay enough attention. Stop seeing with your eyes, children! Grow up right now!" She slammed the cane against the floor, causing Macon to jump. "He will run a game on you 'til it's too late. This ain't a time for games. This here is as real as real spiritual warfare can get."

After those words, Old Lady Lyves was obviously disappointed and disturbed by the interruption. She shook her head, disgruntled and hardly ready to let go of the mission, but she felt in her spirit that she had to let it go for a while longer. "You shouldn't have walked inside if you're bringing panic with you, shouting at me. The devil like confusion, and you see it in here." She then glanced at Macon. "You need to get ready because you're not ready yet. Finding a head doctor, I know, is still somewhere in your thinking, but just remember, it will only subdue that there problem, not cure it, if they don't make her worse off. She our kind, and I can't 'member no head doctor being good to us, not never, like I say before. Make us live worse than dogs in there, like muts. In the meantime, ain't no healin'. Just remember that…it ain't no healing. Don't be distracted no more. Now, walk over here and give me some sugar 'fore you go down that road. I forgive ya and love ya. You older but too young yet to know better," she grinned.

Both Greg and Macon approached Old Lady Lyves, planting kisses her cheek, however, as they stepped forward, it was Sunni who let loose of her mother's leg and moved cautiously backward, afraid of who was before her. Before they even walked out of the front door, Sunni was already gone. Greg quickly followed behind for fear she would run away as she did earlier that morning. It was Macon who straddled behind, feeling guilty of barging in.

"Mama Lyves, I thought that she needed me."

"The hard part of *surviving* in this here world is by *surviving* what is inside us because it's that thing that could lead to us to our own grave…without even thinking about it. Don't let her lose her mind to it, Macon. Stay on her," she stated firmly while squeezing Macon's arm, "And stay with your heel on *it*." When she let go of Macon's arm, she began to walk down the hallway, her feet dragging against the floor, still bothered by the familiarity of that something inside of Sunni. "I 'member your daddy tell me 'bout when that chile was born, out there near Oaksprings, ain't that right? He was shole glad about tha…"

"No, not Oaksprings. Daddy told you that?"

"Rest his sweet soul, he sure did. Shortly after she was born, when he was still walking on this earth, he shole did. Hate he passed, baby. Tell me she was born up there."

"Mama Lyves? Wait a minute." The old lady stopped and turned slightly to see Macon from the corner of her eye.

"What's that, chile?"

"Sunni was born here, right here in Maze, in his house. I don't believe he forgot that," she explained puzzled.

Old Lady Lyves didn't say a word back and nor did she shuffle one limb on her tired body. Her mouth tightened up and after a long five seconds or so, she locked eyes with Macon.

"Mama Lyves?" Macon called, concerned that something was the matter with her when she didn't answer. "Mama Lyves? Did I say something wrong?" she called again, on the way down the hall, but before she could reach her, Mama Lyves spoke, her beady eyes barely holding back the tears that suddenly began filling them.

"Go on. Do as I say, and lock the door behind you. She was born in Oaksprings, not Maze... can't be."

"Mama Lyves…"

"Get out." She continued into her bedroom and shut the door.

Macon, slightly shaken by the change in Mama Lyves's attitude, still obeyed. Before walking outside, she even checked the stove to ensure it was off, and when she walked outside onto the cracked wooden porch that felt as if it would give way any time soon if it were not for the bricks stacked underneath them, she stood there silently as the birds flew overhead. It was at that particular time that she wished that she had her own mother back as she glanced at Greg tickling their daughter who sat in the back seat. Sunni looked so normal. The fact of the matter was that Sunni wasn't in a safe place inside herself at all, and until she could prepare herself as Old Lady Lyves asked her to do, she didn't know what could potentially happen next.

In the next couple of days, Macon found herself wandering, losing all focus, praying for hours while Greg kept the pace going at his job in order to keep his sanity and food on the table. She could sense, however, that he was not only losing sleep, but also slowly losing control. Both of them were stressed, hoping there wasn't another episode. As far as Sunni, she continued to go to school like it was any other day.

CHAPTER 8

"Macon?" called a voice that startled her as she slept with her head against the brick wall at the side of the grocery store. "Macon? Wake up. Are you alright?"

As she attempted to stand, she slipped and hit her head on the same brick that gave her head comfort for the fifteen minutes that she'd been outside during her lunch break. "Am I late?" Worry escaped her heavy eyelids as she caught her balance, barely able to stand due to being in a daze. He reached over and caught her by the arm so that she could brace herself and then checked her over.

"Are you sure you're alright? It's hot out here, even in the shade, and you're fast asleep. I don't mean to pry, but…"

"I just need some sleep is all. I'm fine, and I'm sorry to get in your way. Thank you for helping me up, but I just need to get back to work."

"Macon, I can help you with your duties today. It won't be a problem."

"No, James. I'm fine. I need to just get back in there so I can keep my job," she stated, frustrated from a lack of sleep and having to save money because most of it was spent on her dreams. Everything was going wrong, but instead of accepting his help, she snapped. "I *need* my job. It ain't a want," she stated in a jab at him, stemming from society and how it wasn't even safe for her to get her child looked at mentally because of her skin color, among all the other problems that were thrown at her whole family for being born people of color. James heard the jab clearly, and it didn't fly above his head at all. Therefore, he took several steps back and addressed what he considered to be an unfair judgment on him and his character.

"Macon," he called, placing his hands in his pockets and looking down toward the ground before taking a courageous, deep breath to face her again. "I know I'm white. Marrying a black woman didn't change that, but I ask that you not to treat me like my ancestors or the rest of my racist family. I need my job just as much as you do…even though I realize that the troubles I have are easier for me than they are for your people, easier for me than for even my own wife or child coming. I understand that my skin, just my skin alone, can get me into places where your skin will shut you out. All my life, I have rejected those racist places, making me a full reject to everyone I grew up with mostly. I'm just trying to reach out to help because what I do understand, even if it's just a little, means maybe I can …"

"I'm sorry," she interjected. "I'm sorry." Then she began walking away from him in order to get back to work. "I've just had much on my mind, and I haven't been getting much sleep," she stated, yearning for the rest she needed but not able to get because she was always lying awake at night listening for Sunni to start talking to someone and running and checking on her, paranoid that she was going to end up missing from her bed in the middle of the night from simply sneaking out of the window or out of the front door. Things got so bad over the last couple of days that she had Greg nail her room window shut, just in case she had an idea to leave out that way. It was taking a toll on them both, but they refused to give up or lose their only child to things going on in her head or as Old Lady Lyves said strange voices of demons. "I'm not looking at you through a clear lens is all, James. My apologies."

"Apology accepted because I know something's wrong. I know it can't be easy thinking that *a man like me* can mean you well," he slightly chuckled, referring to being a white man in the highly prejudiced southern town they live in, "but my ears do the same thing yours do. Just like you listened to me, I can hear you and help you if need be. Like I told you before, me and my wife, we got no friends here we can trust or that feel comfortable being around us too long out of fear, so it would be nice for us to find at least one."

"My daughter's sick," she responded. "I haven't had any sleep praying for her day and night, and my husband is shutting up and shutting down," she continued as she began to weep into the palms of her hand. "I don't know what else to do," she continued sobbing while her coworker felt like he'd suddenly dabbled too much in her affairs.

"Well, uh," he stuttered, backing away while pondering what could possibly calm her down without discussing the details any further. "Uh, since you and your family are going through some tough times, my wife is a great cook, an excellent one. Maybe it would be alright if you...or she could cook us something...you and your family something. She loves to cook. Her mother taught her much, and... and it won't be any trouble. It's always too much for me to eat. I'm certain we could bring it over tonight after work because she's always asking about you now, especially since I mentioned you."

Macon glanced up surprised at the offer and the fact that he'd already spoke about her, obviously in a lauding way. At the same time, she was grateful for his offer which she needed, especially since Braille wasn't ever going to provide her assistance any time soon if ever. Therefore, Macon felt it was the best choice to accept the help she was being offered. Besides, it was a way to gain some much needed rest.

"Normally, I wouldn't intrude on your wife being that she's pregnant, but since you say you have plenty leftover and she loves to cook..."

"She sure does. She wants a restaurant one day, if we can save up. We'll move right back closer to CaseTown, and put it there. And don't mind her being pregnant. When I tell you it's her favorite thing to do, it is her favorite. She overcooks…and on purpose," he laughed, "Even more now that she's pregnant."

"Well, I accept the offer." She reached out to grab his hand. "Thank you. We eat around six o'clock. If you come later, that's fine, too. I'm gonna love to meet your wife, James. Maybe we can help each other," she affirmed, truly believing that she needed someone besides Greg to bond with about many things due to the fact that she'd lost, maybe forever, the only close female bond she had in Braille.

"Well then, I'll call her right now," he stated, excited about the opportunity to finally socialize with others in the community without being judged or afraid. He was also tired of him and his wife always being those doing the asking. For once in a long time, he wanted to be the one helping.

||

"They'll be here in a few minutes, Greg," she called from the bedroom, removing her scarf from her hair and touching up her make-up. The skin underneath her eyes transformed her into an elderly woman instead of a well-rested young woman, but she was prepared to engage with her company well due to the fact that they had gone out of their way for her and her family. "It felt good to get a nap in, me and Sunni, right after we got home. I kept her right in my arms," she sighed, having not been able to get a peaceful moment in her own mind for a while. Her only physical comfort was one that she couldn't even feel, and that was when she was asleep. In between times, she and Greg were planning to fast, easing up on the many comforts of life they enjoyed to prepare to start fasting on Friday night. That way, they had the whole weekend to meditate and pray against the evil coming against their daughter. They believed what the Bible said and what Mama Lyves reminded them of right from the scriptures. It just made more sense to take wisdom from God Who is eternal and to take heed to someone who has lived almost a century on earth in great condition than to hear a young head doctor who was just trying to figure it out. To Greg and Macon, it was already figured out. They just had to do their part.

"Well," Greg started, adjusting his trousers and tucking his shirt in, "This will soon be over.

You hear me?" He turned toward her, sounding more definite than he had ever sounded about Sunni and the whole ordeal. "It's about to be over. Some things let out through fasting and prayer. Mama Lyves was right. Heck, Jesus is right. We will just do what we have to do, and let God do the rest. Sunni will be fine. For now, I thank goodness you were able to get some rest." With his arms outstretched, he lovingly embraced his exhausted wife, passionately kissed her, and reminded her of all the miracles God promised. It was after his last warm kiss that there was a knock at the door, and hand in hand, they walked to the door united, along with Sunni trailing behind. It was seven o'clock.

"Welcome!" smiled a rested yet still exhausted Macon as she greeted a woman who was being ushered in by James. She had nothing in her hands, but she was quite full of baby, and that was enough weight to carry. "We're so grateful for your company," she continued, holding her by the hand to help her inside the home while Greg and James introduced themselves to one another before unloading the food from the car.

"It's so wonderful to finally meet you, Macon." Tears of joy were already bubbling in the corners of her eyes. "I've been cooped up in there all by myself since a little after we moved here. I've been pregnant, so that's definitely not good, I don't think. I need to get out, but can't. I just don't feel quite comfortable or safe anywhere I go," she stated with a strong southern accent, similar to her husband's. "Nobody wants me around, and…"

"Well, you're always welcome here, Angela," Macon interrupted, already making a mental note that she was a talker. "I actually plan on being around much more on your side, especially when that brand new baby is born to you. You may need some time for yourself, and I'll be the one to give it to you," Macon offered as a warm gesture. "Do you have any names picked out?"

"If it's a boy, we'll name it James Jr., but if it's a girl, we'll be naming her Sue-Ann. Don't you think that sounds fairly good with the last name Smith?"she asked without awaiting a reply. Instead, it was Sunni who caught her eye. "How precious is she? I hear she wasn't feeling too well? She must be doing better because she looks fine to me, cute as a button."

Macon's eyes shifted to Sunni, but instead of answering the question on whether or not

Sunni was getting better, she nodded, smiled and reached out to touch Angela's protruding belly. "It looks as if the baby's nearly ready. Any day now?"

"Oh, yes, any day. We plan on having a midwife come over to the house, you know, due to…" she responded, her voice dropping to nearly a whisper as she trailed off in thought, but moments later, she picked up where she left off. "Due to our situation, our baby being black *and* white. There aren't too many of us around here, any of us for that matter, and although times are changing, in this southern town, they aren't changing by that much. James doesn't have many people of his kind that totally agree with his choice in me, and me, I'm just out here alone, mostly afraid to mingle because of what my own cousins told me about how the white folk would cut my child out of me if I make a wrong turn, and…it leaves me just afraid. We should have never moved here for what we thought was more opportunity, but…"

"Don't talk like that. Things are changing for the better each day," she stated although she knew based on the civil rights movements and people dying on all sides that time would change, but it would do so slowly due to so much resistance. "Besides that, I haven't seen any sheets around here ever, not since I've been here. No need to hide out anymore because you have me as a friend out here. I'm from Maze, and so I understand. Let me thank you for the food, and I know you must be hungry now, so let's go into this kitchen to see what these men are doing with this fresh meal you cooked."

"If there's any left!" she laughed, hinting that their husbands might have already eaten everything while they were unloading the car.

As they walked into the kitchen, Sunni was already pulling a slice of pound cake from a plate while James was busy making his wife a plate and laughing with Greg. Before the ladies knew it, to their delight, they were being served. For the first time in days, they discovered that it wasn't sleep they needed. It was time to relax, unwind and see that everything was just fine. Food was still on everyone's plate before there was loud knock at the front door. Greg stood up and checked the window. His facial expression went from jovial to concerned as he peered outside. It was James who stood up from the table next, sensing the change of atmosphere once Greg excused himself. Therefore, he followed him to the front door, assuming the worst due to him and his wife, a biracial couple, showing up where they never had before which left him expecting anything.

Macon, although she felt a sudden uneasiness, continued to be a comforting guest to the new friend in her life that tried to be of comfort to her. However, when she heard the tone of Greg's voice, she knew something was wrong.

"Sunni?" he asked, and just as soon as he said her name, Macon stood from the table and glanced out the window. She saw one of her neighbors in the yard. It was then that her heart plummeted when she heard a shout that only she knew by heart. It was a shout that she'd heard from the time she was young. It was angry and inconsolable.

"Sunni! Sunni, come on. Come here!" She grabbed Sunni from the floor and ran her down the hallway, never stopping to look toward Greg as he spoke at the front door.

"You come outside! You come outside right now! I can't even sleep at night anymore!" a deranged Braille belted from the middle of the street. Macon shoved Sunni underneath her bed and told her to be as quiet as a mouse. Then, she locked the bedroom door on her way out to confront Braille.

James and Angela stood horrified at the scene that brewed outside, but they dared not intervene, especially since they didn't know what was going on or for that matter why. All they heard was Sunni's name continuously and the words cursed and witch that threw them into a whole other atmosphere behind the walls of the home. As soon as Angela heard the words cursed and witch, she turned her attention to the back room where Macon rushed the little girl, and then she began to caress her pregnant stomach.

"You leave! You leave here right now, Braille," she shouted so that everyone could hear her. "You're sick! You just left the hospital, and you're losing your mind!" Pretending like something was completely wrong with Braille was the only thing that she could think to yell to take the attention off of her daughter because the things Braille was screaming were enough to ostracize Sunni for good.

"*I'm* sick? I need a hospital? Did you ask your husband what that child came in my house and did to me? Did you?"

At that, Macon placed both her hands around Braille's wrists and squeezed them as tightly as she could. "You got to look into my eyes, Braille. Look at me!" she strained, taking her tone down to a whisper. "I love her," she groaned as the tears ran down her face and her first cousin stared directly at her with absolutely no emotion. "If you love her like you say you did and maybe even still do, even if you still love me, I'm asking you to please put away this rage. And you know what…" she continued as she straightened herself up and wiped her cheeks dry, "Maybe half of what you say is right. I know…I know I didn't listen at first, but something is wrong with her, and I promise you…I promise you…what happened won't happen again. Ain't nobody trying to kill you. It ain't no man, Braille, I mean it. I promise. Just go home, and I can tell you later. Please don't do this to us."

"I do love her, Macon. You of all people know that, but sometimes, the ones you love are the ones that hurt you, and ain't no family of mine gonna ever do it again," she stated, scorned to the core from some secret abuse that happened to her when she was growing up which she still refused to go in detail about. "Someday, I promised myself that I got to love *me* enough for a change, and I don't care who it is try and hurt me, I was gonna…"

"I know. I know. That ain't Sunni. In her right mind, she wouldn't have done it. I'm sorry about when she came there. It won't happen again. Now please…" Macon turned to face the crowd of people who'd already gathered and started whispering pieces of the story they'd heard to put together their own version. She saw some lady's measuring with their hand the height of Sunni which confirmed that she was the topic of conversation. She could do nothing to stop it. Nothing at all, so she didn't try. She turned back to Braille, but she was already walking back home, no one approaching her as her reputation was not only a great person to be around but a person to never cross. There was no in between.

A couple of men from the neighborhood stood on the front porch with Greg and James as Macon walked back with her head held high. No one was going to make her drop it in shame because there was nothing disgraceful about Sunni, no matter what words had become alive in the air. She passed by them as they dispersed in the yard, she became dissatisfied with the whole night which was supposed to bring relaxation and some laughter, instead bringing fear and gossip.

Once she walked into the house turned and went into the kitchen, fully prepared to explain what was going on to her new friend, Angela, she was surprised when she wasn't there. That was when she heard voices coming from the back bedroom, Sunni's bedroom, that she thought she'd locked.

"Mrs. Angela? I heard what you're gonna call your little girl."

"Well, I don't know if I'm having a girl or a boy."

"If it's a girl, can I play with her? We can become best friends as soon as she's out of there and straight to me."

Angela rubbed her stomach but didn't answer. Instead, she stood up from the bed, away from Sunni, and Sunni stood up with her, moving quickly, nearly rushing toward her protruding belly. Quickly, Angela felt it a mistake to come back to the room as she held her hand out to stop the force from Sunni's body that would have rammed into the child in her womb. It was Sunni who called her back into the bedroom in the first place, right after Macon and

Greg left the house. James advised her that the little girl was fine, but she went to check on her anyway, needing to place her own fears to rest as well.

"It looks like everything is settled down now..." Angela stated, needing to move further away, but not being able to because Sunni kept charging, only being stopped by the palm of her hand.

"Mrs. Angela, you didn't answer my question. Can I play with your daughter named Sue-Ann? Can she hear me?"

"Sunni," she answered, already highly disturbed due to the odd way Sunni continued to push toward her, like she was trying to injure the baby. "I told you, Sunni, I don't know what I'm having. Stop pushing up against me!"

Suddenly, Sunni stopped rushing toward Angela. "It's a girl. I know," she said, her attention locked onto Angela's stomach. She then reached out to touch it. "Because I can see her. The best time to learn somebody is when they first come out."

"Sunni!" Macon abruptly interrupted, "What have I told you about your imagination?"

she asked sternly, quickly noticing how nervous Angela was growing. "This child…as you can see…she says things that can put some people on edge. That lady out there, that was her cousin who is more like an aunt to her." Before she could say anything else to explain away the fiasco, Angela spoke.

"A big imagination? She was hollering like there was some truth to what she says. People normally don't…"

"Thank you for the dinner, but tonight just didn't turn out as planned. I'm sorry, but you all have to leave so I can…"

"No, I understand." She glanced at Sunni and then back at Macon who stood over Sunni like a mother who would defend her child until the end of her own life. "You can just bring my pots back to the job and James will bring them home from there." Then, she reached over to shake Macon's hand. "It's been nice. I'm sorry it was a bad time. And, Sunni, I hope you feel better."

"She will. Thank you."

"I will just see myself out," she replied, feeling slightly unwelcome at the moment but also anxious to remove herself from the odd presence in the home, especially around the little girl.

When she got to the front door, James was re-entering. "James, we need to leave."

"Well, it's alright, Angela, and that's mighty rude, especially…"

"No," she stated firmly. He easily sensed that she was unnerved. "We need to leave. Macon will bring the pots to the job. We have plenty more food at home. Let them settle down tonight. I believe they're a bit embarrassed, and we shouldn't add to it."

Without responding, he took her by the hand and led her outside. As she got into the car, he shook Greg's hand, waved good-bye to those who greeted him and finally left. As they drove, they saw the lady who was hollering on the street.

"Follow her, James."

"What?"

"I said follow her. I want to talk to her."

"Look, Angela…"

"You don't know about this! Nobody does. I don't even know if this is something you've ever heard about, but I just need to talk to her because I can sense it, James."

"What are you talking about?"

"That girl back there. You said she was sick. Sick how?"

"I don't know. I just wanted to help, so I felt…"

"I know what you felt. You felt just how I felt, but what if she's a kind of sick like that woman said she is. What if she *is* cursed?"

"Do you believe that? She's five years old, Angela. Curses and witches? Angela," he sighed.

"I know the stories. I know from someone who knew first hand," she stated, looking back at the figure of Braille as she walked fiercely to her destination. "One thing I have to do is find out…because if it is true…then they're in trouble. Trust me, James. Just follow her. They may be in more danger than you know."

Instead of turning right, he turned left. It looked like she was going across the fields into another neighborhood, so they drove slowly until they reached a turn that would take them towards her. Moments after they turned on one more street, she was there, storming with every footstep, her hair undone and her clothes as if the footsteps of many children stomped the wrinkles in.

"Don't come with me." She unlocked the door as the car crept down the road.

"Wait. What are you doing?" James asked frustrated as he brought the car to a halt, unlocked his door, and got out. "You can't just jump from the car like that, Angela."

"Don't!" she shot back at him as if he'd offended her when in reality, he'd done nothing wrong and he knew it. Instead of following her, he looked down at her round belly, got back into the car and slowly followed behind in the vehicle. Before Braille entered her house, Angela yelled out.

"Ma'am! Ma'am! Excuse me," as she wobbled forward, taking Braille by surprise. "May I speak to you for a moment? I heard you back there…and what you said…" she paused, glancing back at James who immediately stopped the car once more. "Can we talk?"

Braille didn't answer. Instead, she stood in front of her door with a blank expression as Angela drew closer. She paid no attention to the car that lingered behind the strange woman approaching, but she was on guard to fight for her life if necessary. The only thing she needed for the fight was her fists, teeth and legs, and that wasn't going to change.

"What do you want?"

"I want to ask you about the little girl named Sunni."

"Who are you?"

"My name is Angela. We heard you screamin' back there. I'm from Maze. I see you looking back at the car. He's my husband, so he's nothing to worry about."

"A white man is your husband?" she asked with a pause. "Here?"

"I know."

"Get out my yard. You just being nosey." She turned away from the woman, believing that what she said would shut her down and make her give up on finishing the conversation.

"Well, it's actually *you* who wanted everyone to know your business since you were shouting it all in the streets anyway, so my nosey really isn't nosey at all."

Braille's hand remained on the doorknob, but she didn't turn around again to face her. Instead, she gave her a firm warning. "The only reason why I don't strike you now is because you pregnant. Leave." Shoving the door open, she stepped inside, but before shutting it, Angela spoke something into existence that took control of Braille's mind.

"She's gonna kill you." Angela just stood there in the deafening silence as the sun started going down, but when Braille didn't return words, she spoke again. "She's gonna really kill you. You have to leave here, but if you don't die before she is able to find you, she will kill you then."

Braille stormed from the door and towards Angela, and as she did, James jumped from the car and ran her way. However, Braille was already nose to nose with his wife before he was able to keep them apart.

"You let me tell you something. I done sat in that house for weeks, barely getting any sleep, sometimes scared outta my mind, but one thing I won't do is run from the only thing I got left on this earth. I ain't got no husband, and I ain't got no white one either who can move me from place to place. One thing I got is what I know, and I know ain't nobody coming in here to kill me without a fight…including Sunni!"

"You've got to listen to me!" she shouted, attempting to grab Braille's wrist as she walked off, but Braille clinched her fist and swung to knock her hand away. It was James leaped in front of the blow.

"Keep your hands off of me! The only one you better restrain is Sunni…since you know so much." She stormed back into her home, slamming her door so hard that the windows shook. This didn't keep Angela quiet.

"As soon as I heard your voice out there, I saw it," she called after her, knowing that she was inside still listening. "I saw it with my own eyes, Braille. She's gonna wait until the perfect time because there aren't many times that are perfect. She'll be before you and take your life just as clear as I speak. You won't see it coming. Just remember that. You won't see it," she stated as she began to cry as if it had already happened. "The devil has a way of setting things up!" she shouted in one last ditch effort. Then, she turned hopelessly to her husband and whispered, "I can't help what I see, James."

"Get in the car, Angela, now. She could have killed you herself if you knew how my shoulder felt from the blow I just took to it." As he opened the door for her, he complained, "You should have told me you had a vision. You really should have told me before this."

Meanwhile, inside the home, Braille stood at the edge of the window, examining the entire situation outside until they drove off in their car. She didn't leave the window at that point, but she only stood there until the sun drifted down out of the sky. It was when the darkness rolled completely across every portion of the sky did she retreat to begin her ritual of placing marbles and jacks all across the floor for anyone who decided to break in.

||

"I don't wanna talk about it," she stated, tossing all the food in her own bowls in order to prepare for clean up. She'd lost her appetite in the midst of all the hurled insults toward her child that she simply didn't want to breathe anymore unless she was alone.

"Baby, listen…"

"I said I don't…"

"Listen!" Greg shouted. "It's the truth! She said nothing but the truth! Running away from the truth won't help it any, and we know that. Sunni walked over there and tried to kill her, and that's it. We can't defend that, but we can defend Sunni. We did and are still doing that. You hear me? Now, let's stick to the plan. We are gonna eat, and after that, we are gonna fight a good fight!" he continued, slamming his fists into the table. "I feel just like you, but I got one mission in mind here, and after that, we can go on. You told me not to break, so you don't either. Sunni!" he called. "Get up here and eat this food." He walked toward the refrigerator to get a drink of fresh lemonade from his favorite cup. "If we break in front of all these people, it's over. Hold your head up, and we will show them the end of it."

They all sat down at the kitchen table and ate, slowly starting to speak to one another about everything except for what just occurred. After eating, they both tucked Sunni into bed and went their separate ways, Macon into the kitchen once again to clean up and Greg to the backyard. He stood there against the brick in the darkness, seeming to only be staring at all the stars in the sky, but he was praying. His chest began to quake, and as he slid down out of the moon's view, he strained from his heart silently while the heavens looked down upon him and moaned, "Jesus, help my baby. Help us, Lord, please. Don't pass us by. If You just see us...please." He never came back inside, so Macon met him where he was. They both cried out to God with their tears together for strength, realizing that many times things get worse before they get better.

CHAPTER 9

"I don't know." She slid her shoes off before heading back to the bedroom quickly, feeling the need to wash even though she'd already done so hours earlier.

"Don't tell me what you don't know. You knew a lot based on the conversation that I heard. Stop... Angela...don't shut the door in my face."

"I'm not, James. I just need a minute to wash up. I have to wash."

"You just washed! What is going on?" He threw his hands up in the air, walked into the bedroom and sat on the bed. As he removed his shoes, he thought of how the night he planned for relaxation and building a bond with someone outside of the home turned into a nightmare. "I don't believe this," he complained as he threw himself backwards. He stared at the cracked, white ceiling and followed the crack to the wall where he traced that same crack all the way down to the floor. Shaking his head, he laid there until Angela walked back into the room.

She said nothing nor did she look James in the eyes. The home was warm, so she turned on the fan to cool down while she changed into her night clothes.

"Are you just going to walk around me like I don't need to be informed of what is going on?"

"The little girl. While you were outside with Greg and the others, I was back there with her. I went back there because … well, I just needed to go back there, check on her," she said as she sat on the bed. "She was crying when I walked in, and we talked. That's when I got that feeling."

"What feeling?"

"The feeling I always get when I know something, the truth of something." She turned to him. "She has an evil that takes over her. She was even … was talking about our baby. Said it was a girl inside me."

"What? What you're saying makes no sense," he frowned in confusion. "It's a little girl with probably some bad habits that did something wrong."

"It's not her, James," she whined. "You have to trust me on this. How many times have I had this same feeling and been right? Answer me."

"Since I've known you."

"Well, this is the same thing, except much stronger, and I never claimed to be a prophet but God shows me what he shows me. That's what makes it right…when it comes to pass."

James stood up from the bed, paced in front of the closet and finally asked, "What did you see?"

She raised her head slowly. "I saw Sunni kill that lady." Shaken, she continued. "She never saw it coming, even though she thought she would be prepared. She wasn't prepared at all."

"Where?"

"I don't know where. I saw it. When God shows me these things, they're like riddles or in signs, like puzzle pieces that He explains to me in my spirit, not in words. I wake up knowing, but this wasn't a dream like most times. This was a vision as she was talking, it was like God just poured it in me, and I saw it. I'll know it when it happens, but only when it happens … or is about to happen. I will get that overwhelming feeling like something is wrong but familiar. They're not safe."

"What can we do about it?"

"Pray. When it's about to happen, we need to pray for intervention. We need those angels that the Lord says He will send. That day, we will need them, or nothing will stop this. God already gave the warning to me, and He gave it to me for a reason."

"We can just tell Macon and warn them…"

"They won't believe us. Nobody ever believes me. I don't look like God speaks to me, look at me. People have never listened, so I stopped telling. I would just watch things happen. They only listen to full out preachers, and I ain't never had a robe nor a pulpit. I'm too normal. The first mocking thing I ever heard when I told somebody was *why would God only tell you*? That's when I became afraid to tell…because I never knew the answer to the question. I really don't know why God chooses to tell me. He just does."

James took her by the hand. "I'm gonna try, try to tell her what you told me. The worst she can do is never talk to me again. If she does listen…"

"She won't." Angela kept the rest of her knowledge of the situation to herself, but while she remained silent about those thoughts, there was the beginning of peace coming to the home of the McKinsey's in the form of sleep, something they'd become deprived of and thankful for more than any other time in their lives. Unfortunately, at the home of James and Angela Smith, something disturbed the night, waking Angela up.

Angela rose from the bed as her husband slept soundly beside her, his body lying atop the covers as usual due to the humidity indoors. The windows were open, but while there was nothing unnatural about the scenery, there was something very abnormal about the night. The sweat caused her pajama top to stick to her skin, so she removed it and put on another as she searched the room for something she felt but couldn't see. Terror gripped her spirit as she spun around the room, needing to scream but not able to make much noise except for covering her mouth while inhaling and exhaling.

The car keys were on the nightstand, and even though she shouldn't leave without James knowing where she would be going, she didn't want to chance him stopping her. She swiped the keys from the stand, slid on a gown and rushed from the house. The time was two-thirty in the morning when she drove away from the home, and it was two-forty five when she arrived at her destination.

The car remained running as she stepped from the car and hurried to the house, her face covered in tears. Her fists banged on the door as the rain began to fall across the rooftops. She stared into the night sky as she awaited an answer while the sky began to speak in its thunderous voice.

"Open the door!" she finally shouted, kicking the bottom of the door with her feet until it finally flew open. Both Greg and Macon yanked her inside the house, quickly shutting the door behind her and barricading it from whatever they thought was after her.

"Where's James? Is he alright? Are you alright? What's wrong?" Macon asked as Angela leaned her back against the wall and wailed as if she was in labor. "Are you in labor?"

"Macon, get her!"

"Angela, calm down," she calmly stated as she went to her knees while holding Angela's hands, believing she was talking about her unborn child about to drop from her womb. "Come on down here with me to the floor," she continued. "Where's your husband?"

"No, Macon! Oh God," she wept. "Please go get her. She's not here. Your daughter...she ain't here! I saw it again. Please!"

"What? You saw what?" Macon asked as Greg placed the last chair at the front door to stop the intruder he felt was after Angela. He stepped back and listened to her closely, trying to decipher what sounded like a riddle to his ears, until he finally took off into the back bedroom.

"Macon," she cried apologetically, "I'm so sorry I didn't tell you, but it's happening tonight. Sunni ain't here. I saw her...you gotta believe me. I saw her kill Braille. I saw her about to kill your cousin. This same dream, first it was a vision. I saw it twice. Two times...and it woke me up, please you gotta help me pray..."

"Sunni..." Macon whispered under her breath but she was nowhere near as calm as she sounded. She was already up off her feet as Greg was coming back up the hallway.

"Macon, she ain't here," he stated, shoving his shoes on his feet and getting his car keys.

"What? No…no, no…" She ran past Greg and into Sunni's bedroom. The sheets were already thrown back to parade an empty bed, and when she fell to the floor to look underneath, the shoes and dolls smiled back at her as if they were alive and enjoying their mocking. "Sunni!" she shouted, running through the house, turning things over and tossing clothes from the closet that purposely became a shield from her daughter.

Finally, she ran outside, passing a praying Angela who was still on the floor, and jumped into the car with Greg who was already pulling out of the driveway. Angela lifted her head as the car pulled off. The car lights were bands of light flying in the darkness through her teary eyes, and as the red lights faded, she wiped her eyes to see a figure standing in the rain. She stood up and walked forward, wiping her eyes to be certain about who she was seeing. It was Sunni. She was smiling at her from outside in the rainy darkness. Then, she lifted her hand and pointed at

Angela's stomach while walking forward until her finger pushed against the screen door.

Angela met her at the door and held the screen door tightly so that it wouldn't come open, and as she did, she felt a large amount of water down her legs and onto the floor. Sunni pulled on the latch, but Angela wouldn't allow her to open it. Their eyes met as Sunni began to speak.

"She's mine. She's all mine."

"Get away from here!" Angela screamed as she shut the door, locked it and fell to the floor. "Oh God, please send your angels, Lord. Please…" As she spoke, she felt what she recognized as her first labor pain, and she grabbed her stomach. Scooting against the wall, she used it to hold her up to search for a phone, but another labor pain came right after the first causing her to bend over in agony. "Help me!"

"Braille? Braille? Open up! Braille!" Macon screamed as she shook the handle on the door while Greg hit it with so much force that she even thought the door would cave in. "Sunni!"

"I'm going around back to her window because if Sunni is doing the same thing she did last time, that's where she is."

"Oh dear, Lord! Braille, please!" The rain pounded the house until the front door unlocked. "Greg! Come back!" she hollered as the door opened to Braille standing there with a knife in hand, ready to attack.

"Why you banging at my door this late at night?"

"Braille, put the knife down. It's me…Macon."

Braille's eyes were bloodshot, and she'd become even more paranoid ever since her encounter with Angela. She heard a sound coming from the side of the house. When the footsteps approached, she saw that it was Greg, and she lifted the knife higher.

"Both of y'all coming for me?"

"We aren't trying to hurt you, Braille. It's Sunni. Is she in your house? Is she here?"

Macon pleaded. "Put the knife down, Braille, and let me in. She's missing. She's not home."

"Ain't nobody here but me," she stated but just as those words of assurance left her mouth, she second guessed herself because she had been asleep, therefore, may not actually know if anyone, especially Sunni, was inside with her. "Come on in here," she said, moving the knife to her side but never letting it go. "Check. If you find her, get her outta here. I'm headed to the back. You two search up here, then we switch."

"Wait…Braille," Greg stopped her by grabbing her wrist. "You gotta give me the knife. You're not stabbing my daughter," he promised, shaking his head. "I understand how you feel, but I won't let nobody hurt her, not as long as there is breath in my body. Now, let me and Macon get her outta here if she's here."

Braille snapped back. "You let go of my arm! Ain't no way I'm letting go of this knife. I can swear to you though, that if I find her, I won't kill her, but I'm keeping this knife on me. If you don't like it, leave. This *my* house, and she ain't come to kill you like she did me."

"Don't hurt my child," he warned.

"But you let her come and hurt me."

At that, they searched the house, even searched the backyard, but Sunni was nowhere to be found. There weren't many places to hide in the small area, but as they stood around and thought about where she could be, Macon went back outside the door. "Greg, come here. Maybe she went back there," she suggested, referring to the woods. Then, she looked at Braille who then nodded her head in agreement.

All three of them left the house, locking the back door behind themselves, however, they'd forgotten to lock the front door. Sunni stood there at the front screen as they walked out the back. Then, she let herself inside, locking the screen door behind her.

||

"I'm taking you back home," he stated whipping the car around the corner since there was no sign of Sunni in the woods where they searched.

"Why? No...no. I need to look for Sunni. It's in the middle of the night, and she's out here somewhere."

"We don't know where she is as of right now. She could be already back home, but you need to be there in case she shows up."

"Angela is there, Greg," she stated firmly going against his suggestion that she should just stay put while her flesh and blood is out roaming the street, possibly out of her mind. "I'm not staying. We need to stay out here…"

"You go back home and call the authorities. Stay there until they come because she isn't where we thought she was, now is she? We need help lookin'. If I can't find her, I'm gonna wake up some of the guys down the road to help me look. You need to be there for the police."

"And how long you think that's supposed to take, for some police? What do you think they will do? Angela saw it first. She was right! Sunni wasn't home. Why shouldn't we take Angela's lead right now since she knew more about Sunni's whereabouts than us?"

"Well, she was wrong about one thing, wasn't she?" he shouted, tired of the weight that continued to knock him down at every turn. "Was she there? Was she at Braille's house?" he yelled again. "Was she there?"

"No!" Macon shouted back. "No, she wasn't, but that doesn't mean anything. She got a gift, Greg. She knew!"

He pulled into the driveway, leaned over and unlocked her door. "You're staying. Do what I ask, Macon, please. Get the police. You and Angela can look around closer to the house. Ain't no telling how long Sunni been out the house."

Macon, furious after his demands, got out of the car as to not stall the search and watched him leave the area, but as she walked closer to the house, she heard screaming from inside. "Angela?" The front door was shut and locked so she banged repeatedly as Greg was already down the road and didn't see that she was locked out. "Angela, open the door!" Within seconds, she heard the door unlock, and she rushed inside to water all over the floor and Angela on her knees wailing so loudly that she immediately knew she was in labor. "Angela," she called as she fell to the floor with her. "You're having your baby now. You got to lay back and open up."

"No!" she screamed, grabbing and squeezing Macon's arm. "No, I can't have her yet. It's out there. It knew my baby was coming."

"What? What are you saying? It? What it? Stop talking in riddles, Angela, and just say it!"

"Sunni came to the house. It knows I'm in labor and needed to draw you all out of the house. It used me."

Frustrated, Macon shouted, "Angela, just say it!"

"It's the omen! Nobody spoke of it. It was forbidden. You… you didn't hear about it, did you? You have no idea."

"No. Maze is running rampant with superstition, and…"

"Well this isn't fake, Macon! This one is real, and it's as real as the flesh on your body. They didn't want to scare us, so they didn't tell us. They believed that not repeating it would make it die. It did die…until now." She moaned as another labor pain rolled across her belly and back. "They kicked her out of the town, the lady that had the issue with what they call demons. They kicked her out, wouldn't let her stay."

"Who? Who is they?"

"Just listen!" she continued, breathing deeply in order to tolerate her pains. "Girls born to the ladies who casted the woman that was filled with demons out of the town for fear, it would be their future generations of daughters born in Maze who would suffer from the same demons she had. You and me, we were already born, just too little to understand much plus they decided not to tell any of us. It was against her own fears and promises, my mama let me know…she told me the truth about why I should never have my babies there in Maze because of this same omen that's over that place. Why you think people take their wives to that place on the outskirts of the border to have children if they can't make it to the hospital in the next town? You never thought that was odd?"

Macon fell back onto the puddle of water on the floor, shoving her body away from Angela slowly. She paused all movement when she heard the next question.

"Macon, you have to tell me, where was Sunni born?"

The silence answered for her, and she began to shake her head slowly against the memories that matched everything Angela said, causing everything that didn't make sense from her childhood to make sense.

"Macon, your mom had to be one of ones, like my mom, who participated in driving her out without helping her through her troubles. It caused the evil to grow stronger, angrier and more hateful than it ever was."

||

"Take her! Just get her! We have to put her out of here before day break."

"Now?"

"Yes, now! We have families to raise, and all she does is walk around here terrorizing everyone. It's not good. The other day she ran up on Lilly Bee's porch and took hold of her child, didn't she?" she asked, tugging on the lady's arm in question. Lilly Bee answered the tug with her head held high and unashamed of how she grabbed a broom and chased the possessed woman off the porch.

"I sure did. I would've beat her 'til she let loose of my child if I would have had to, but I didn't. One lick, and it was over. She has to go."

Another lady in the group of about twenty chimed in. "Yes, it must be done, and there's enough of us right now, while we're having this get together. She's just around that corner in that old abandoned house. We can use this to cover her mouth," she said, holding a plaid scarf in the air, "but we got to put her out of this town and make her understand we mean business."

"I brought a gun. Took it from my man's coat."

"A gun? I'm not killin' nobody. I got a family to raise, and I ain't a murderer. All we need to do is tie her up and put her out of here. She's always knocking on people's windows and chasing us…" a terrified woman stated who held her arms together like she was in the middle of a snow storm when it was actually a little over seventy-five degrees outside."

Finally, another woman stepped up. "We don't need a gun, and we don't need to hurt her. We just need to scare her out. All we need to do is put the fear in her, and she'll go. There's no need to do much else. Nobody wants to be where they aren't welcome, and I as one know that even though she's crazy, she got enough sense to stay away where she's been run from. Lilly Bee, has she been back to bother you on your porch?"

"Nope, lesson I hit her again with my broom. She just walks by…scratchin' and gnawing at herself. Just completely out of control. I never seen anything like it."

"See. Now, that's all. Grab some rocks and even though we wanted it to be silent, it won't be. Make a lot of noise. People will join in, so be ready. Don't touch her. Just run her out. The more people come out of their houses, the better."

Someone else walked in to join them. It was a lady named Sunny. "I heard what you said. As long as we don't hurt her, we need to get her out. She's nasty. Using the bathroom on herself and trying to do it on others as well. I don't know what happened to her. She wasn't always like that…talking to somebody who ain't there."

238

"That's why she got to go. Our ancestors know what that is, and we can't forget. She a witch and done been took over by that evil and she wants to take our children. She eats but not food. She eats flesh, even her own. The devil done got inside her and made her just like him, now we got to get her out of here so we can be safe. Witches ain't welcome. She hexed, and she wanna eat the weak to stay alive." Then she spun around to look everyone in the face. "What if we aren't there for our children one day, when we aren't looking? What then? They go missing, and we find them? The only answer to that not happening is to get her out, with all her hexes and laughter and staring…she like to scare me to leave from here myself."

"One day, she walked up to me like a normal person. She even smiled at me, made me think she was back to normal, but as I nodded my head and walked by, she turned back to follow me, step by step. I even felt her breathing down my neck. When I turned around to hit her, she caught my arm and stood there. Then she said, "I'm just looking at you." When she let me go, I ran my fastest. Been scared of her ever since. She's harming us on purpose."

"She wasn't always like that though. Something happened, so until she returns back to how she was, she needs to go before she hurts one of us…"

"She has. Nobody still knows what happened to that girl. When the police came, she sat over there in the fields, rocking back and forth, smiling. It was her. I know it was."

"There's no sense in talking. Let's get her out of here."

The chase began. On the way to the worn down house, with no electricity or even a bathroom, the group of ladies walked down the road in silence at first while some people who were on their porches looked on, wondering where they were headed. They found rocks and sticks, even pine cones, to throw in case they needed to throw them, and as they approached the raggedy home, the door opened wider as it never was ever completely shut. The woman whom they called crazy and demon possessed named Carver came out.

Her hair was wild, and her skin was filthy as she stood there underneath the full moon pulling at her face like she wanted it to come off. Then, she suddenly stopped yanking at her cheeks to look at the women who came to visit, startled as they eased toward her. That was when the shouts began, but instead of running back inside the shack, Carver leaped forward like a wild animal, demanding they back away. In the same breath of anger, she began laughing and ripping at what little bit of clothes she had on.

The crowd of women then began to shout in a rage, angry at how the woman had tortured the grounds where they lived. Soon, their husbands began to show up and even teenage children following behind them to get the woman out of the town of Maze for good. A witch was what they called her, and she began to be spit on and knocked with rocks as she fled down the main road to her exit. As she neared the end of the road, the woman fell to her knees and began to crawl, and the tears that had begun to fall from her muddy skin had already dried up. Finally, as she made it to the sign that boldly read, *Welcome to Maze*, she turned and cursed them all in a fit of laughter.

"I will still have your daughters and their daughters so long as they be born in this town, I will be inside of 'em," she yelled, beating her chest. "Because of what you did to me, I won't ever rest but will walk the streets and take them at my own will. You can't chase me out! This here is where I be born," she scowled.

Then crazy lady Carver laid down on her back at the border of the town and laughed until there was no more laughter left. Some women fled immediately, distraught by what the woman cursed them with. At that point, they feared, believing that they'd made things far worse than what they already were. Those with children, especially girls, ran off while the men stayed behind, insuring that the woman didn't cross back into Maze. It was Sunny who stayed back behind a tree and watched as the woman stayed on the ground cradling herself in laughter although nothing was funny. It was as she stood behind the tree watching that Carver lifted her neck and turned to the right to stare directly into her eyes.

Frozen, Sunny moved out from around the tree and stared back at her. It was then that she knew for sure that putting the woman out of the city wasn't going to fix anything. There was something sinister inside of her that could see beyond what a body could see. Quickly, after breaking from the hypnotizing gaze, she ran. She ran as fast as she could run in full regret of what she'd done with the other women of Maze. They had fought the wrong fight. What made matters even worse was that days after leaving Carver to the wilderness beyond Maze, she was out to market in the next town and saw her on the way there, leaned over into the side of the road. She was picking weeds from the ground, shoving them into her mouth like a sick dog would do to make himself feel better. As she passed by her in the car, as if Carver knew she was there, she looked up from her, and her eyes landed directly on her as the car passed by.

Carver's face was covered in scratches and dry blood. She appeared like a woman who hadn't slept for days, but as Sunny leaned out the window back at her, Carver lifted a sign that was laid out on the grass behind her that read, "Help me." In an instant, heartbreak shot through Sunny's heart as she then faced forward in the car while the driver continued without a thought about what had just occurred. Being filled with remorse, she fully gave up everything she once believed in, superstitions and all and gave her life fully to the Lord, causing her to rush back to the spot where she saw Carver weeks later, however, she never saw her again until the day she was found dead, all cut up from self inflicted wounds. She knew that they'd fought the wrong fight. The fight they should have fought was a spiritual one.

On that day was when everyone who participated in casting out Carver chose to remember what Carver said vividly. They all promised to keep quiet about it to keep the torment and fear from spreading from generation to generation. Therefore, began making up lies of great fortune to persuade their own expecting daughters to go to the better spot, a spot they built up on the outskirts of Maze, called The Birth House, for women to give birth to their young. Other women, the ones who came to believe only in the only true power of the Lord, chose to simply not speak of what happened but also never participate in The Birth House lies to cover it up. Sunny was one of those women, choosing to teach the power of Jesus over any curse because whether Carver's omen was real or fake, it would be only God who could defeat it anyhow. Therefore, she shielded Macon from it and all the new superstitions taught until the day she died because the only way to defeat a bad spirit was with the Holy Spirit.

All of the ladies and the men back then who knew made a pact never to utter what had been called Carver's Curse to anyone unless it was truly necessary. If the story died, it would die. That was the belief. That was the goal – to somehow turn a bad into a good through deception. It took no time for The Birth House to become the most desired place for women to deliver.

The women kept The Birth House freshly decorated with flowers and completely stocked with everything necessary for birth after it was built. It wasn't a fancy building on the outside, but it contained all the frills on the inside, built on land that had been passed down as heir property to one from the community in the neighboring town that didn't mind the place being there at all. Whenever someone needed to deliver, it was the place they would get to early enough, at the first sign of pain. The place was decorated so beautifully and comfortable until all of the younger ladies the next generation never asked about why it was built because it seemed for obvious reasons – just a secluded, comfortable place to give birth with the midwives. The older ladies who knew the secret remained glad of this believing that it was fixed, believing that they had outsmarted Carver's Curse through changing the narrative.

||

"That's the real truth about why we leave, even if it is right outside the border of the town in that house they built…the one they call The Birth House. Nobody was gonna tell you. My own mom wept like a baby when she told me. She thought she was letting something out again. It's to contain the curse from those being born. It wasn't built for any other reason than that. If we don't help Sunni, it's coming for my baby."

"How will it get to your baby?" Macon whispered. "We aren't in Maze. Your baby should come out well enough now, won't it?" she asked puzzled by the riddles.

"No. I said they *contained* the curse by not letting any babies be born in Maze. Through your daughter who was born there, it made it out. We have to stop it from getting mine because my mom was just as guilty as yours. My baby don't stand a chance."

"And Braille? Why try and kill her?"

"Because it wants to kill her to hurt you. If it gets inside my baby, it will target someone else I love. It loves suffering, and it was set out in vengeance to devour those who changed its original course -those people and their future. Don't you see yet? It's an evil spirit, and it's only jobs are to inflict loss, destruction, and death. From what I learned, this one is one of the most aggressive. There must be many kinds, but Jesus said *this kind* doesn't go out except by fasting and prayer. Macon, I may cook much, but I'm a regular faster, and I pray all the time."

A giant pain made its way from her abdomen to the small of her back, and as the pressure came like an ocean to the hard ground of a deserted beach, she leaned back in agony as the storm within her raged to exit. "You gotta pray with me, Macon. It's the only way to stop it. You ain't gonna find Sunni right now because it's waiting on mine! Sunni is the distraction, and if my baby's body is almost ready, that means if we don't pray together right now, your baby might not ever come back. There's no telling what that demon will have her do next, just like Carver. This is the only way to save her. We don't have much time. It's ready to move."

A rush of raw emotion and agony befell Macon as she couldn't deny any part of the story that Angela said. Things all made sense. She thought back to how her mother casted out all things that tried to set themselves higher than the power of God, and she even remembered how she would watch as her mother shook her head when women would walk to The Birth House while they were screaming in labor sometimes. No one passed the story to her, not her mother or her father, because no matter what the evil, they believed it could be destroyed with the power of God. Macon had never had to fight like this. It was all brand new.

Macon's tears dried up. "They should have told me."

"It was forbidden. It was only when your daughter said what she said to me, I felt her illness. I knew I had to tell you after God showed me all the pieces to the puzzle, so please, we need to help each other. Grab my hand before I can't do this anymore."

Macon looked toward where the telephone was and the thought came to abandon everything she just heard, but as she sat there, she heard the voice of her own mother and Mama Lyves. Her decision was made. She turned, grabbed Angela's hands, and they both began crying out to the Lord for Sunni's deliverance from the evil curse. The thunderstorm roared, the humidity hovered, and Angela's womb quaked for relief. Meanwhile, right across the grassy field, a little girl had already entered a house and hid like a child playing an innocent game, except nothing about her hiding was innocent nor was it sport.

Braille, tired but unable to go back to sleep, sat down on her aged brown, plaid couch, left to her by older relatives who didn't need nor desire it anymore. She loved sitting in it because it would remind her of a time when she was full of company, all around her and loved. It was only in her recent days that she felt shunned and alone, misunderstood and though powerful, very powerless. Although she'd walked around town with a face full of life and boisterous voice, she felt the exact opposite. She couldn't stop the downtrodden way she felt, and she didn't know any other way to be even though she tried. She had no one, and her mind kept people away.

Each day she walked out the door since Sunni changed, she yearned to see the only family that loved her. She wanted to laugh and talk with her only friend and closest cousin, but her mind wouldn't let her. Every time she tried to calm down, she got confused and even more afraid, ending up falling to the floor, trying to squeeze the troubles from her mind and act like everyone else for once in her life. It had never been like that, but it was Macon who'd always tolerated and loved her, almost thinking her personality fairly funny most of the time.

She started crying as she sat and soon placed her head into the palms of her hands and rested her head on her knees. Deep in her soul, she knew she was right about Sunni, but she didn't know how to stop her without hurting everyone else. Braille's mind was simple, and in times like these, her mind was never her best friend. Rage was. No matter what, she was always protected there, and she didn't recognize any other way to express herself if it didn't start with a loud strength. What nobody saw, however, was how she really felt – heartbroken – especially because she may have to one day kill her own baby cousin.

After finding a way to console herself as she had been used to doing for most of her life, she inhaled deeply and relaxed her eyes, closing them, in an attempt to concentrate on moving on the best way through her life with no help. Her water had gotten shut off two days ago, and the only way she got water was from the rain. There was large tin bucket on the outside catching everything the Lord sent her way. She wanted to ask someone for help, but she was tired of doing that. She wanted to try once again to hold things together on her own, regardless of situations, so people wouldn't look at her as just strong and odd, but strong and smart.

She exhaled and then inhaled once more, and as she stood, her eyes closed and arms raised high in a full stretch as to ease some of the tension that had been building for days, she finally opened her eyes to gather a small slice of relief … until there was a real, physically painful slice carving into her right abdomen that cut so deeply, when she looked down, the blood was already pouring out. A girl stood there holding the knife. It was Sunni.

The sparkle of the moon reaching in from the window left and darkness fell upon Sunni's face while horror seeped into Braille's soul as the knife came back once again for another slice. It was at that moment that Braille's fist went across her young cousin's face, knocking her to the ground as the knife lightly slit her stomach once again.

Sunni hit the floor and didn't move as the knife flew from her hand. A stunned Braille refused to move one inch as she forgot about her own wound, observing how still Sunni was on the floor. The rage and horror she thought would take her through disappeared, and tears fell from her eyes at the lifelessness in her baby cousin. She went down to the floor as her own blood emptied onto the floor like it was coming from a pitcher to a glass. Then, she lifted Sunni from the ground and limped toward the rainstorm outside her front door.

As she passed beyond all the ornaments and accessories that her mother left her that was passed down from the old land to keep evil away, she realized that not one of them worked. The evil still got inside her house, so as she walked, she viciously kicked them from her path. She didn't believe in them anymore. As she looked down at the niece that lie there in her arms motionless after the blow to the side of her head, she began walking beneath the thunder and through the muddy fields as the blood left a trail of grief behind her.

‖

"I can't breathe, Macon," Angela panted. "Move me outside. We got to keep praying, but help me outside. Quickly, help me outside. I need some air…"

Macon shoved the screen door open as she heaved Angela outside of the hot house. The wind wrapped it's arms around them, and the rain pounded their skin as Angela couldn't hold the baby in any longer.

"Macon! Macon, leave me and lift your hands to the heavens for my baby. If she comes right now, she needs to be free. Leave me now!"

Macon turned and fell to her knees as Angela screamed, and the rain fell. Then, she lifted her hands to the heavens shouted a praise to God that seemed to make the thunder go silent. She begged for deliverance from all the evils that surround them, including that evil that was inside of her child, and she sealed the praise and prayer in the name of Jesus. The rain continued to pour, so heavily until it was hard to see even three feet away, and as nature took its course, a baby was born.

"Macon!"

Macon turned around, and suddenly, so much pressure left her soul as she looked down at a beautiful, newborn baby. Quickly, she ran into the house, grabbed a knife, and ran back into the rain to cut the cord so that she could run the baby back inside to get dry and cleaned out.

As she cleaned the baby and wrapped it in a towel as the wetness ran down her body like a fountain, she placed the baby down directly in her line of vision at the doorway and headed back outside to help Angela.

"Come on, come on…she's fine. She's fine," she stated, leaning over to place Angela's arm on her shoulder.

"Macon…"

"Come on, you can do it. We got to get out of this storm, and I can barely see in this night. You're bleeding, probably all over the yard and…"

"Macon, it's over," she stated as Macon tried to lift Angela from the ground. "Turn around and look. Look beyond the rain."

She removed Angela's hand from around her shoulder and turned around to look behind herself to finally see the outline of two figures. There was Braille. She was carrying Sunni.

"I'm sorry," Braille broke down, trembling and holding a lifeless Sunni in her arms. "What I believed back there only killed her, Macon, but ain't nobody but Jesus can bring her back to life. I don't want her dead no more, Macon. I hit her too hard...and I'm so sorry."

"Sunni?" Macon mumbled in utter disbelief at what stood before her underneath the once petrifying storm that suddenly wasn't as intimidating anymore. Her tears wrestled with the rain pouring onto her skin as she drank the words that came from Braille's mouth as if they were a callously prepared poison. Thousands of invisible palms felt like they were pushing her further and further away from the realities in front of her, but as she drifted off, about to fall to the ground, it was Angela's voice who woke her up.

"Bring her back! There is life tonight! There will be no death. I haven't even seen my own baby yet," she shouted powerfully through the shrieks of catastrophe in the middle of the muddy, bloody ground, "But I won't go in there to even look at her until Sunni is back. Whoever the Lord touches even once is set free, now wake up, Macon, and get your baby just like you got mine."

It was those words that made the penetrating invisible force of thousands of hands shoving her away feel more like flakes of sand that could be blown away with an infant's sneeze. She remembered what her mom told her days before she left the earth to be with the Lord. She explained faith to her.

Faith wasn't what you see. It was what you believe beyond everything else. She said that a shaken person doesn't have faith. Just like an unborn baby with no cord can't breathe, a person not connected to faith is without life and life eternal. A person must connect to faith just like that unborn baby to that umbilical cord or there was no way that miracle can take place.

It was then that Macon's mother took her hand firmly, very tight, like something was on her mind for a long time and said "*I am praying to God that you will have faith because you will need it. Once you have it, you will know because it is the substance or touchable, real item, in things you hope to have making it the evidence that it is so, no matter what you see with your eyes. What you hope for is actually real because what is real is right there wrapped as a gift in faith. Put away all else. Just have faith.*"

"Give me my child," Macon spoke.

"Macon, I'm sorry."

Macon walked over and lifted a lifeless Sunni into her arms with all her tears dried up. She realized at that moment that she had nothing to cry about when she had the answer in Jesus all along. "Ain't no devil gonna cause the death of my Sunni…not when there is God." She didn't go into the house at all, but instead, she dropped to her knees right next to the new mother, and they clasped hands over Sunni in the pouring rain, coming together in prayer for her life. Five minutes went by and then ten as the child's body was drenched in rain, but as their pleas got louder before the Lord, Macon finally felt Sunni's chest rise. She flinched backwards, lifted Sunni into her arms and sobbed, "Thank you, Jesus. Thank you, Lord."

Angela fell backwards, extremely weak, wet and full of emotion for the miracle that had just been given, and as she began to crawl back to the front door to meet her baby, she heard an ambulance coming down the road. Then, she looked near the driveway. Braille wasn't there, and it was that which made her heart begin to race again.

As quickly as she could, she made it through the front door to see her living, breathing daughter, swaddled up tightly and still breathing. She gave her a kiss, but she knew something was wrong. As she scooped up her newborn, she took one step forward. That step was enough to reveal Braille, lying on the kitchen floor slumped over with the telephone in her hand. She then saw the bleeding wound.

"Oh, Jesus… Macon! Macon! Oh dear God…" When Macon didn't come through the door, she yelled again, until she heard footsteps come through the door. It wasn't Macon. It was an emergency worker first then came Greg seconds after. As soon as the emergency worker saw that Braille was in the most distress, he ran back out the door to retrieve more items while Greg took Angela and sat her down on a blanket. Then, he got another blanket for both Macon and Sunni, wrapping them both as tightly as possible before questioning Macon about everything that was happening.

"Greg, not now. We can't talk about it now because of them…" she stated cautiously until she saw the unexpected. "Braille? Oh my God, Braille!" It was her first time seeing her cousin since Sunni came to, and she had no idea why she was being carried out lifeless from her house. She even saw the blood through the sheet. Greg swiftly took Sunni from her arms as Macon fought to grab Braille's body, but the emergency workers pushed her away.

"She's still alive. We have to go."

"No," she wept. "No…that's my sister in there. That's my sister," she stated as she fell to her knees, her emotions completely out of control and mentally in a fog. Within seconds, there was another ambulance turning the corner in the pouring rain, and when they pulled up, they were alerted to get Angela and the baby. The next to pull up was the police, and Macon froze. She watched as the ambulance left with Braille, and then she followed each step the police officer took to reach her front door.

She turned around and watched as Greg stood tall, held Sunni tightly in his arms and walked toward her. Then, he reached down and stood her up by his side. The officer was a tall, built white man, and he had a younger officer who ran after him, ducking in the rain. Greg opened the screen door and let them inside.

"Thank you," the officer said. "Mighty wet out there."

Greg didn't say a word, but only held his daughter tightly, like he knew that any second they would try to pry her away.

"Is everything settling down over here. We got several calls of a commotion, screams and we need to know what was going on so we can write a report."

"Our daughter went missing, but we found her. She likes the storms, so she runs out in them, and this one happened in the middle of the night so…we apologize for the noise but our neighbors know us, and we don't know why they would call…" he stated unaware of all that transpired.

"Got a runner," the officer smirked, making a joke that wasn't funny to Greg nor Macon. "She looks asleep now."

"She is," Macon blurted. "She's not used to being up this late. Glad she was right outside. She had us terrified for a second."

"And these ambulances?"

"A pregnant friend who came over here to help us look for Sunni. Like I said, we panicked. She ended up breaking water right here under our feet."

"Oh this ain't rain water I'm standing in?"

"No. She had the baby right in here and out there. See the blood?"

At that, the officer tipped his hat and walked out, irritated that his shoes were all mixed in water and blood. "Y'all have a good night then," he stated as he threw his hands in air, jogging back to the car with his partner. "I stepped in that stuff…"

Greg shut the door to Macon's horror stricken face. "They're gonna come back for my Sunni," she stated as she pulled her from Greg's arms and fell to the floor thanking the Lord for all He'd done.

"You heard the man. Somebody called and…"

"Sunni was dead. Braille, she walked her down here." Her eyes fell low.

"Dead? Braille? We went to Braille's. What you saying?" he asked, clearly befuddled and in disbelief as he began to breathe erratically while looking at Sunni sleeping as if she had never been awake the entire night.

"I know we went to Braille's, but Angela was right. She was right. God speaks through her. She told me to pray, so we prayed out there. Right out there," she pointed. "My baby wasn't breathing, Greg. Braille hit her so hard, but Jesus let us have her again, and that means she's not sick anymore. Whoever He touches, they come clean. She's clean, Greg."

"Wake her up," he stated, reaching out to grab her. "Give her to me. Where did Braille hit her? Sunni?"

"I don't know why she's not talking, but…"

"Sunni! Wake up."

It was then that her eyes opened for the first time since her death. After she opened her eyes, she looked at her mother and father, then slowly drifted back to sleep. They remained awake all night, holding her in their arms, waiting for the sun to dry up all the rain and overpower the dark night.

SUNNI'S REBIRTH

"It's going up in the air! Keep runnin'! Keep runnin'!" Greg smiled as he watched Sunni run with the colorful kite on a warm, breezy day while they all sat out in the backyard of Braille's home. While Greg took off after Sunni, Braille and Macon sat on some metal stools silently as they watched him never take his eyes off of her.

Macon looked over at Braille with noticeable sincerity, "Thank you," she stated as she reached over and grabbed her hand, squeezing it tightly while the thick bandage that covered Braille's knife wound shown through the shirt.

"I ain't never been perfect, Macon, but ain't no way I was gonna tell them who cut me up...not after what I felt after striking her. She ain't move, no breathing, and it was the first time I felt bad about protecting myself. It was the very first time. I regretted..."

"I know. That's just how you are and have always been. It's not your fault though. I know what you been through, Braille," she responded mercifully. "You're still my sister though…cousin…and I love my Sunni," she sighed to catch a glimpse of her laughing with her father. "But not many people would blame you for what you did, so don't blame yourself. Something else was in her that's not there anymore. She sleeps soundly at night, and there are no troubles since Jesus touched her."

"Macon?"

She turned to face Braille. "Yeah?"

"Do you believe Jesus will heal my mind, too?"

"It's not a matter of if I believe. All that matters is if you do. Trust me, what you believe is all that matters. Keep praying, but most of all, keep believing. You see our living proof in front of your eyes. Just look at Sunni go."

Even to this very day, the superstition and lies surrounding The Birth House and Carver's

Curse in the town of Maze have been replaced with truth, faith and Sunni's Story.

THE END

Thank you for reading An Evil Was Born. If you enjoyed this book, please leave a book review as your review helps push good vibes about the story and author. Your read and review is very much appreciated. Thank you for your support.

Please find and read more books by Mirika Mayo Cornelius at mirikacornelius.com.

.

www.ingramcontent.com/pod-product-compliance
Lightning Source LLC
Chambersburg PA
CBHW031939240626
47153CB00003B/786